When Thunder

Rolls

The Mile High Series #7

By Aria Grace

When Thunder Rolls

Published by Surrendered Press

Chapter One

Josh

The yard is larger than most we've looked at but so is the price tag. By almost double. "Babe, I'm just not sure we can swing this."

Matt doesn't seem to hear me as he picks up a tennis ball near the deck and tosses it across the yard. "Sure we can. You've got the money from your grandpa. It's not like it's helping us by sitting in the bank."

I turn back inside so he can't see my frown. My dad's dad did leave me some money when he passed away last year, but I hoped to save some of it. Put a little aside for a nest egg. "But five fifty is a lot."

"But the basement alone is worth it. We could have some killer parties down there." Matt lightly smacks my ass as he passes me to check out the basement one more time.

It is an amazing house. Two hundred thousand dollars more than we can realistically afford kind of amazing. "I'm just worried about the monthly mortgage. If we put everything we have into the down payment, we'll be screwed if we have an emergency."

Matt turns on his heel and reaches for my hand, pulling me against his solid chest. "Once we set up the studio in the garage, I'll have more clients than I can handle. I'll have to turn them away." He leans forward and kisses me hard on the mouth. "You have nothing to worry about."

Those six words always make me a little nauseous. When I was nine, my dad said them to me the first time I rode a bike on my own...and I ended up knocking out my front tooth. And when I had a concussion from a street hockey accident the morning before I took my driving test for the first time, the DMV instructor said the same thing. I couldn't concentrate and almost got us killed by running a red light. And the night my best friend in college told me she had breast cancer but the doctors were optimistic it hadn't spread, she used those same damn words to stop the flood of tears flowing between us.

The same sense of foreboding hit me then that's hitting me now.

This is when I need to start worrying.

~**~

"So, are we making an offer?" Matt is fooling around with his phone while I make breakfast. "Because that place is gonna go fast."

I flip my omelet and choose my words carefully. "Actually, I don't think we can. We aren't qualified for that much, and I just don't think we should commit everything we have. With the wedding and honeymo—"

"Dammit, Josh." Matt tosses his phone on the table and plants both palms next to his plate. "Why are you always such a pussy about making decisions? We've talked about this a hundred times. There is no risk. I'll make the mortgage payment on my own if I have to. You just need to get us into the house, and I'll handle it from there."

God, I want to believe that. I know Matt believes it'll be that easy, but I'm just not sure. Matt comes from money. He was raised on an estate, and his family has homes around the world. He doesn't completely understand what it's like not to have enough. His parents practically disowned him when he joined the military and hate that he's gay. But he's still chasing their approval, even moving our wedding date to October so it would accommodate their travel schedule.

He thinks that if they see that he's happy and successful, they'll forgive him for everything else and release his trust to him. They throw him bones now and then. Like buying him a sixty-thousand-dollar truck for his birthday and agreeing to pay for our honeymoon to Fiji. But really accepting him back into their lives? I just don't see it happening.

And since I'm the only one with a job, the loan will be in my name. That means I'll be responsible for the full payment, whether he contributes a dime or not. "But you only have three reliable clients right now. What if you don't get more?"

"Oh, I see." Matt folds his arms over his chest and leans back. The tattoos covering his bulky muscles never fail to turn me on, but I'm so frustrated right now that even his sexy body doesn't distract me while he rants. "So that's what it comes down to. You don't believe in me. You've never been supportive of my business, and now you think I'm a fucking failure. Is that it?"

I turn off the stove and go to him, pulling up the chair beside him so I can sit close. "Baby, you know that's not true. You can do anything you put your mind to."

Matt cuts me off again, jonesing for a fight. "But..."

"But, personal training is a competitive industry. People use apps and YouTube to work out on their own these days. I've been doing some research, and it might take a few years for you to build up enough clients to pay the bills."

"You've been doing research?" Matt pulls away from me and stands up. He hovers over me like he wants to punch me, but he thinks better of it and pulls back. Just because he works out every day and is ex-military doesn't mean he's a bully to me. At least not usually. But he's been a lot more volatile lately. In fact, that's what got him discharged dishonorably from the army.

Matt has always been one to throw punches first and ask questions later. I knew that about him when we met, but he's never raised a hand to me, and I believe he never will. I'm a little ashamed when I flinch at the sound of Matt's fist bouncing off the table. "You know, if you really want to marry me, you're gonna have to have a little more faith in me."

"I do have faith in you..." I have to leave for a four-day shift in less than an hour and really don't want to have this conversation. Again. "I just want us to be realistic. If we get a smaller house, that'll leave us with a much bigger savings account."

"The smaller houses are all shit." Matt storms out of the kitchen toward the bedroom.

I consider following him, but he needs a few minutes to cool off. And I need to think of a new argument. Honestly, it's not just about the money. That's a big part of my problem with the house, but the bigger issue is the house itself. It's too big. We don't plan to have kids, so three thousand square feet for the two of us is just too much.

Besides, the house I've been drooling over for the past three years is finally on the market and exactly in our price range. A gay couple bought the dilapidated cottage about ten years ago and fixed it up to be my dream house. There's a picket fence in front of a perfectly manicured lawn. And a wooden swing hangs above their front porch. They even have a line of fruit trees in the backyard that I'd kill to get my hands on.

But Matt hates that house. I think the detached garage would be perfect for his studio, but he doesn't think it projects the right image to his clients. And if he had more than two clients, I might agree that bigger might be better. But right now, I'm just wondering if we'll even make it to the wedding with all the fighting we've been doing.

Just as I finish eating, he walks back in with his laptop in his hand. "I just gave notice that we're moving out. We have forty-five days to get into a fucking house or we'll be homeless."

My jaw drops and that rock in my belly expands to fill in all the corners. "Are you serious?"

"Of course I'm serious. I'm tired of waiting around for you to shit or get off the pot. Someone needed to push this process forward, and it sure as hell wasn't gonna be you."

"But, Matt..." I don't even know what to say. How could he do that without talking to me first? What happened to being partners? "Why?"

"If you don't like that house, fine. We can keep looking." He places both hands on my thighs and bends down so he's looking me square in the eye. "But we are officially on a timetable here. If we aren't in contract within the next two weeks, we'll be living in the truck."

My mouth hangs open as I try to come up with a response.

"So I suggest you get that cute little realtor of yours to show us a few more places...pronto."

When Thunder Rolls

CHAPTER TWO

TYLER

I sit and stare at the bright yellow publish button for five full minutes, mentally going through a checklist of everything that needs to be done before I push it. Once I do, it's out of my hands and open to public scrutiny.

I get like this every time I finish a new book. I always feel nervous that I haven't proofed it enough or removed all my notes to myself. And I can't help but be self-conscious of the fact that people might hate it.

I take a few deep breaths, swiping away the blond strands hovering over my eyes, and push the button that officially sends it out to the major online retailers. There's no turning back now. A few thousand people have preordered copies, so even if I wanted to stop the presses, I can't.

This is happening.

Right now.

And since my file won't be editable for the next thirty-six hours, I need to stop worrying about it. What's done is done. With a determined flick of my wrist, I close my laptop and head to the kitchen for a celebratory cup of coffee.

"Honey, you look like shit." Mom peeks over the top of her steaming mug with her loving words of maternal encouragement.

"Thanks." I can always count on her for honesty.

"Did you sleep at all last night?"

I shrug and prepare my cup of cream and sugar with coffee. "Not too much. Definitely not enough."

She shakes her head and turns back to her oatmeal. "Seems like clockwork. Every two months you have these sleepless nights. You have some kind of man-struation cycle happening that I don't know about?"

I smile at my mom's bluntness. "Shut up," I say playfully, trying to cover up my surprise that she's been paying such close attention to me. She might as well be keeping a calendar because she's exactly right.

Every time I finish one book, I set up my next book to publish exactly sixty days later. I had no idea mom was keeping track of my publishing cycle. Of course, she doesn't know that's what it is. I've been writing for the past two years, and nobody knows about it. Not a single soul.

My tax accountant is the only person who knows that the unknown author of a best-selling suspense thriller series is actually me. I write under the pseudonym Rex Calloway because that name is much more butch than Tyler Kelly. Besides, I don't exactly like to be the center of attention. At least, not in a professional sense. I'm fine with all eyes on me when I walk into the Unicorn on Saturday night, but that's different. That is me looking for a fuck. I've never gotten a bad review on a fuck and don't expect I ever will.

On my books, that's a different story. Although the books do extremely well and earn more during a release month than most Americans earn in a year, there are still haters out there. Although I've never confirmed or denied it in the books, the rumors on the chat boards and fan sites about Jaxon, the main character in the series, being gay have created quite a bit of controversy. At some point, Jaxon will find a partner of some kind. But for now, my fans are forced to focus on the stories...not a love interest.

When my first novel debuted, I quickly shot to the top of all the major bestseller lists. I was even more shocked when the book I was selling for less than five bucks a copy yielded six figures in its first month of release. I considered telling Mom when that first paycheck arrived. But something held me back. And now that I've had seven subsequent release months just like that, I feel like it's too late to tell her.

I don't want her to think I was trying to keep that part of my life away from her...but that's kinda what I was doing. I just needed something for myself. Something that wasn't for her or the bookstore or the house. Something that was all me.

And now I don't know how to tell her.

After my dad died when I was nine, I had to step up and be the man of the house. And since I'm the most twinkish guy I know, it hasn't been easy. But life isn't always easy. So when Mom needs me, I'm there. I didn't even consider college beyond my associate's degree in business administration. I would have been happy to skip college altogether, but Mom insisted I have some of the traditional college experience. I just hated being on campus when I knew she was running the store by herself.

Now that I'm here full time, Mom is finally starting to live a little too. She's even wearing makeup again and has started power walking. If I didn't know any better, I'd think she was trying to spruce herself up for a gentleman caller.

"Is it that grinding porn or whatever they call it?"

I almost spit my coffee across the room. "What are you talking about?"

She waves her hand at me as if to shoo away a fly. "Oh, don't get all shy with me. I'm your mother. I know you meet up with men from that app. I listen to the radio."

"You heard about Grindr on the radio?"

"Yes. The hosts of my morning show, Maddie and Erik, they're very progressive. They've taught me a lot about the world you millennials are living in."

Dear god. "No, Mom, I'm not staying up late with the grinder porn." I laugh and try to hide my embarrassment behind my mug.

"Well, whatever it is, I just wish you could take care of it during normal hours so you can get some sleep."

I nod and let the subject drop. It's only on days fifty-four through fifty-seven that I really pull all-nighters. So, I'm not too worried about the other fifty-three days of the month when I sleep just fine. Once I upload the final copy three days before it's released, I'm free…

"What are you up to today?" I ask as she gets up to rinse her bowl.

"Kim is working till two, so I'll probably just run some errands today. I might pick up a roast and get it into the Crock Pot if that sounds good to you."

"That sounds great." I glance at my watch. "Oh, I need to get going too, but I'll see you in a few hours."

Mom walks over to me and presses a kiss to the top of my head. "Have a good day, honey."

"Yeah, you too."

My mom bought the bookstore a couple years after my dad died. We moved in to the house behind the store when I was twelve, and I've been helping her run it ever since. I was living in the apartment above the bookstore for a few years after college, but it didn't make sense for her to be alone in the big house when we could both live there and collect rent for the apartment. Besides, she's a great cook, and I was at the house every night for dinner anyway. It works out pretty well for both of us, but it does mean I can't bring guys back home. Well, I can. I just don't like to.

Mom's always been 100% supportive of me since I came out when I was fifteen. But I still think it's awkward to parade lovers in and out of the house when she's home, especially the ones from Grindr that I'll never see again. I wouldn't want her to get attached to anybody who won't be sticking around.

After inhaling a couple slices of toast, I jog across the yard and head to Owl Eyes Bookstore, my mom's pride and joy. Kim opened up at eight, but I don't like to leave her alone for too long. It's a safe neighborhood and we've never had any problems, but some of those old books feel like they carry ghosts.

I've been creeped out on several occasions when I was alone in the store. Especially at night.

"Good morning, Kim," I say as I pass her. She's shelving go-backs in the kid's section.

"Hey, Ty. Morning."

"Anyone in here?"

She shakes her head and turns back to the books. "Not right now. A few people were in earlier, but it's just us at the moment."

"Okay. I'll be up front." The building is technically two stories, although half of the top floor is a separate apartment and the other half is more of a loft. Bookshelves line all four walls and a railing is set up about four feet away from it so people can look down to the main floor.

We mostly carry new and antique books, but we've recently added consignment books from indie authors. That's how Rex Calloway's books ended up tucked in among the traditionally published books.

Just as I slide my coffee mug behind the front counter, my daily dose of hotness walks in. Chad is a firefighter who comes to the store pretty regularly. When he's not looking at car magazines, he's looking at fitness books. And without him realizing it, I've even managed to get him hooked on my Glass Bay series.

"Hey, Ty. How's it going?" he asks as he leans an elbow on my counter.

"I'm great. What are you doing out so early today?" Chad usually doesn't come in until early afternoon.

He raises his Starbucks cup to me in explanation. "Yeah, well, just getting off my shift and needed some caffeine. It'll be a few hours before I can go to sleep, so I figured I'd see if that next book has been released yet."

My smile on the inside is huge, but I try to maintain an expression of indifference on the outside. "It gets released in a few days, but I probably won't get copies until next week."

"Yeah, all right. What else you got for me? I've officially run out of reading material, and I can only look at the stuff with pictures for so long before I start to get sore." He waggles an eyebrow at me to make sure I catch his drift.

I chuckle and walk out from behind the counter. "Yeah, yeah. You know, you can get helpers for that kind of thing. Just this morning, Mom was telling me about the Grindr porn."

Chad bursts out laughing. "Your mom said that? Dude, what did you say?"

"I just laughed. What can you say to that?"

Chad stretches out his fingers as if working through a cramp. "Oh, I know all about the Grindr porn too, but when I'm in the firehouse for four days at a time, I need something a little less offensive to read in front of everyone else."

"How about this?" I point to a new release that's been getting rave reviews. "I think you might like it."

Chad grabs a copy and skims the back, nodding his head in approval. "Yeah, I'll give it a shot. I'm gonna go check out the magazines. I'll be up in a few minutes."

"No rush." I turn and head back to the counter at the front. "Take your time."

Chad is a good guy. When he first started coming in, I tried flirting with him. I wanted to make it clear I was interested if he was. Unfortunately, when he never responded, I got the message loud and clear that he wasn't.

But banging a firefighter is still on my bucket list, so I'm not giving up hope for us.

Chapter Three

Josh

"You getting up or what?" Chad calls across the room, smacking my foot as he passes by.

"What time is it?"

"Time for you to get your ass out of bed. We have a meeting in twenty minutes."

"It's six forty?" I bolt up out of bed and search for my phone, immediately regretting the sudden movement as a wave of nausea passes through me. Fuck, I feel like shit.

"Yeah, you forget to set your alarm?"

"No." I toss my phone on the bed then stand up, stretching out my aching muscles. "I think I hit the off button instead of snooze about an hour ago."

"Loser."

I rub my eyes and realize he should be getting ready to leave. "What's going on? Why can't I sleep?"

"Cappy just called a meeting. Sounds important."

"Great. I'll be down in a sec."

I quickly get dressed then brush my teeth, not bothering to do more than run wet fingers through my wavy brown hair to work out some of the bed head.

"Don't worry, princess. You're still the belle of the ball," Dwight says as he passes by the bathroom.

Everybody likes to tease me about my hair routine. It's not that I'm vain, but if I don't spend more than a few seconds on it, it turns into a big fluff ball. Matt is always bugging me to buzz it like he does, but I just can't bring myself to go that short. But days like this make me reconsider my commitment to having something to hold on to.

I barely have time to grab a bagel before Captain Mulder whistles to get our attention. He goes through the standard morning updates, and I'm only half listening until he mentions the annual Toys for Tots program.

This year, our station is hosting the event for the entire city. We'll be organizing the donations for all the fire stations in Denver, as well as coordinating distribution to the nonprofits that will match the toys up with needy kids.

Maser clears his throat and asks the question we're all wondering. "Hey, Cappy. It's still August, right? Why are we talking about this now?"

Cappy gives him an annoyed glare before turning back to the group. "In the past, we've just had to put out a couple barrels and make a few appearances. But as I just explained, we're hosting. That means the program doesn't happen unless we make it happen."

He pauses for a moment to let that sink in. "Last year, we didn't start pulling in donations until October, and as a result, we were short almost ten thousand toys."

"What's the goal this year?" Chad asks, stepping forward. He's always been a big supporter of the program.

"We're expecting one hundred thousand requests this year. That's almost double what we saw last year. And since we were short last year, it's gonna be tough. We need to reach out to the community early and often so they don't get complacent." Mumbles and groans fill the spaces of silence while Cappy takes a breath. But he quickly shuts down the murmuring with a raised hand. "If you know anyone with a business that can donate, hit them up. If you know someone with storage space we can use for a few months, don't be shy about asking. I don't plan on telling a single child there isn't a toy for them this year. We're not the biggest station in this town, but I believe we're the strongest. We can pick up the slack others have left in past years. Are you guys with me?"

Cheers and whistles erupt in the room. I didn't grow up wealthy, but I always had food on the table and plenty of toys under the Christmas tree. I can't imagine what it must be like for the kids who won't get anything.

Captain Mulder waits just a second before speaking again. "Now, in order to make this happen, I need a few volunteers. A small team will serve as liaisons between the businesses that'll host drives, and another team will help coordinate the drop-offs to the organizations that'll distribute toys to the kids."

I know better than to raise my hand. It's a big responsibility. I'm not surprised when there's nothing but crickets in the room. Everyone wants to help, but being on a special team is a lot to ask on top of our regular duties for the next several months.

"Should I just start picking names?" Captain Mulder asks, waiting for people to step up.

Dwight clears his throat and slowly raises his hand. "I'll work with the nonprofits."

"Alright, thank you. Looks like Forrester actually has some balls and recognizes an opportunity to impress the boss when it's presented. Anybody else?"

"Yeah, I'll work with the businesses to host drives." Chad always takes on a leadership role, so I'm not surprised to see him volunteer.

"Excellent." Cappy turns to the rest of us. "Now, the rest of you need to pick a job and connect with Forrester or Ludwig by the end of the week. I want to know you're all doing your part this year for the kids of Denver."

"Yes, sir!" Several voices sound at once before we're dismissed.

I'm just thankful I didn't get stuck with any of the major responsibilities. I love these annual toy drives and have a lot of fun watching the kids open presents, but this just isn't a good year for me. Between buying a house and planning a wedding, there's no way I'm gonna have time for a big project like this.

As soon as everyone starts to clear out, I head straight to Chad. "Hey, I'll help with whatever you need. Just let me know what I can do."

Chad gives me a half nod and a smile. I know that means he'll be dumping a ton of shit on me as soon as things start to get really busy for him. I just hope it's all after the honeymoon.

The day drags on forever. We have several inspections scheduled, and as the hours pass, I feel worse and worse. Whatever caused me to sleep in this morning is messing with my head and stomach. By six in the evening, I'm puking like my insides are trying to escape my body.

"Fuck, what the hell did you eat?" Chad steps away from me and covers his mouth and nose when I finally emerge from the bathroom.

"I think it's the flu." Everything hurts, and I can't think straight.

"Well, take that shit home. You don't need to be spreading your bugs to the rest of us."

I hate leaving mid-shift, but I can't work like this. And it would be irresponsible to risk getting any of the other guys sick. "Can you get someone in to replace me?"

Chad nods and ducks around a corner. "Yeah, I'll make the calls. Just get out of here. Can you drive?"

I groan and hold my belly for a second. "Yeah, I can make it home."

CHAPTER FOUR

TYLER

After taking a few hours off in the middle of the day, I come back at five to finish my shift. Whether I open the store or not, I'm usually the one to close it. I don't like Mom having to stay late every night. She's still young and very active, so I know it's not overly taxing for her to work long days. But the woman is fifty and deserves to have her evenings to herself, especially when she's putting a delicious meal on the table for me.

Darren is working the front when I walk in. "Hey, Ty. How's it going?"

"Good. How are things here?" I ask as I approach the front register. After hitting a few keys, I pull up the sales for the day on our point-of-sale system. Not bad.

"It's been good. We've had a steady flow of customers all day long. I even had to start a waiting list for the new Rex Calloway book. Apparently, we're the only store in town that sells his paperbacks, so his fan club wants copies as soon as we get them."

"Really?" I smile but try not to giggle in excitement at the prospect of having such loyal fans. It's moments like this when I wish I could tell the world that it's me. I'm Rex Calloway. I'm the author of the series they've grown to love.

But I feel too much guilt over having waited so long to share the news with people. I should have done it as soon as the first book hit the bestsellers lists. And although I don't like to think of myself as superstitious, I almost wonder if I'd be jinxing myself by sharing my secret. Like, if people know it's me, maybe they'll start hating the books. Or worse, I'll start writing shit that I wish people didn't know was associated with Tyler Kelly.

All I can do now is show my excitement on the inside and give myself an invisible pat on the back.

"Yeah. People love those books." Darren was one of my first fans, although he'll never know it.

"That's cool." I turn back and take a few moments to calm my giddy energy. I'm often hyper and excitable, but I don't have much experience with holding back my emotions. It's an attribute I haven't quite mastered yet. I clear my throat a few times too many before turning back to Darren. "Is anyone here now?"

Darren looks up and nods toward the children's section. "Some woman with a little kid is reading back there. They've been here for about an hour so she might be getting ready to check out soon."

"Okay, I'll go check on her in a minute to see if she needs any help."

Darren glances at his watch. "Are you ready to get started or do you need to do anything before I take a break?"

"I'm good. You can do whatever you need to do."

His wide grin is adorable as he leans back and pats his stomach. "Marge said she's got a pot roast with my name on it if I want to stop by on break."

"Yeah, go ahead." I should have known food was involved. Mom is notorious for feeding her employees. "But I'll be over in about an hour so you better not eat it all."

Darren raises his hands as he backs away from the counter toward the back door. "No promises, man. I'm a growing boy."

I shoot the rubber band I've been playing with at him but he ducks before it makes contact. I'll get him on the way in.

~**~

With the store quiet and not much left to do for the day, I open up my laptop and start outlining my next book ignoring Darren when he returns from eating my dinner. I have a couple storylines in mind but nothing concrete yet. I'm just jotting down random notes and ideas when I hear a small cry from the children's section.

Several people have come in and out of the store since I arrived, but I don't remember anyone with young kids. I leave Darren at the front and head toward the children's section to make sure everything's okay. There's a young woman curled up on the floor in the corner with a toddler in her lap. She's flipping through a Shel Silverstein poetry book. It's a big book, and they're three-quarters of the way through it. I wonder if she's actually been reading every page or skipping around. Either way, it looks like they're here for the long haul. "Hey there, is there anything I can help you find?"

The woman startles and folds her arms protectively around the little girl in her lap. "Yeah, we're just reading. Is it okay for us to be here?"

"Oh yeah. Of course. You're fine." I take a step back to appear less intimidating. "I just wanted to check and see if you need anything."

"No, we're okay. Thanks." She gives me a small smile and adjusts the child in her lap.

The baby has a pacifier in her mouth and sucks faster as she looks at me with wide eyes. "I'll just be up front. If you need anything, you can holler."

I'm not sure if the woman is the mom, the nanny, or the sister because she looks young...like high school young. But they seem to be fine, so I leave them to their reading and go help Darren with the small line of customers who have gathered at the front to check out.

~**~

At 8:45, I flash the lights twice to let any lingering customers know that we'll be closing in fifteen minutes. A few minutes later, the young woman and the toddler emerge from the children's section looking exhausted. The young woman peeks out the window and seems a little concerned.

"It's really coming down out there," I say, glancing out the window. "I hope you have umbrellas."

The woman looks outside again and then at her phone. "Um, you close at nine, right?"

"Yeah. You've got about ten more minutes."

She looks around and notices the few customers still shopping. "Can we stay here until you lock the doors? I'm waiting for someone to pick us up."

"Yeah, of course." I'm certainly not gonna send them out in the rain any sooner than I need to. The little girl starts crying. After a panicked look in my direction, the woman digs into her pocket and pulls out the pacifier.

"Shh, shh." She tries to soothe the baby by bouncing her in her arms. "I know you're hungry. I'll find you something soon, I promise."

The words don't sound like something a typical mother would say to a child. She didn't say they'd be home soon or that she would be buying dinner. She said she would find something. It's not my business to interfere but something in the desperate tone of her voice, and her hollowed out cheeks makes me concerned about letting her step out into the storm.

"So, do you live around here?" I ask the woman while sending a text to Mom.

Can you bring some leftovers to the store? There's a customer here waiting out the storm who might appreciate a snack.

"Yeah. We stay a few blocks away. My boyfriend got off work about an hour ago, so he's probably just stuck in traffic. You know how the roads get when it rains like this."

Sure, honey. Any requests?

Something suitable for a toddler.

The roads are a mess. Several customers commented on the accidents they passed on their way in. "Yeah, I'm sure he'll be here any minute. I've got some work to do on my laptop, so I don't have to lock up right at nine."

When Thunder Rolls

CHAPTER FIVE

JOSH

I manage to make it home without puking in my lap, but that's only because there's nothing left in my body. At this point, all I can think about is curling up in bed and hoping death comes quickly. It's twenty to eight by the time I finally walk in the front door.

Matt isn't home, but that's not surprising. I was only two days into a four-day shift. He probably made plans with a client or friend. I call his cell phone but am sent straight to voicemail. "Hey, babe. I'm sick. Just wanted to give you a heads up. Love you."

Instead of going straight to my bedroom, I veer left and head into the guestroom. Our little rental is small, but there's a spare room that has a decent bed in it. Instead of contaminating our room and maybe getting Matt sick, I crawl under the covers of the guest bed without even taking off my jeans or hoodie.

I don't know how long I'm out before bright lights shining through the bedroom window wake me up. It takes me a moment to realize where I am. The digital alarm clock on the nightstand says it's three thirty, but that doesn't seem possible. Matt would've woken me up when he got home. Unless he didn't want to disturb me. Although, Matt isn't usually that considerate, so I have to wonder if he came home at all.

The lights get brighter, and I have to shield my eyes as I sit up. Through the rain-blurred glass, I see someone pull up in my driveway. The car is too small to be Matt's truck, and worst-case scenarios immediately run through my mind.

Was he hurt? It's raining pretty hard out there.

Was he in an accident?

Without even slipping on my shoes, I rush through the house and tear open the front door to see who's here. The storm has rolled in, and it's coming down in sheets, reducing visibility to just a few feet in front of me. I hear the distant rumble of thunder a few seconds before a flash of lightning illuminates my worst nightmare.

It's not a state trooper coming to tell me that my fiancé is hurt. It's another man, wrapped around my fiancé, kissing him with a passion I've never witnessed in real life. I take a few steps forward then stop, frozen under the raindrops engulfing me.

Matt and his friend are completely oblivious to the fact that they're soaking wet while they continue to devour each other.

Minutes or hours pass, I don't know which. All I know is I can hardly catch my breath as I watch my whole future dissolve right in front of me. The stranger finally pulls away from Matt and walks to the driver side door of a small sports car. Matt just stands there in the rain, watching as the car backs out of our driveway and eventually disappears down the street.

The grin on his face is wider than I've seen in a long time. Matt seems to unconsciously rub his hand over his crotch, giving himself a good tug before he looks up and finally sees me standing in the rain. He stops midstep, watching me watch him. He doesn't even pull his hand away from his dick as his smile slowly fades.

I can almost see his mind working to come up with an excuse. I know him well enough to know he's searching for some way to justify what I just witnessed. But he knows this is a deal breaker for me.

From day one, I made it clear to him I would never share.

We would not have an open relationship.

I would not allow someone to disrespect me in that way.

My stomach is in knots again but not from my flu. With a completely stoic face and a firm voice, I force out the only words I can manage tonight. "I'll open the garage door." I hold his gaze, not giving him a chance to say anything. "Take your truck, and get the fuck out of here."

"Josh, babe—"

"No." I shake my head, and the tears I hoped wouldn't fall do. Masked by the falling rain, I don't try to wipe them away. I just glare at the man who, up until just a few moments ago, I thought loved me. "I'll have your shit put in storage and let you know how to pick it up, but don't ever come back here."

Matt's fists clench and unclench, and he opens his mouth a few times as if he has something to say. But each time he closes it...not bothering to insult me with a lie.

Good.

I have nothing more to say to him, and there sure as fuck is nothing he can say to me at this point. Without another word, I turn around and walk back inside the house.

Alone.

~**~

Between the shock of seeing Matt's true colors and the fog of my achy head, I barely have the presence of mind to drop my drenched clothes on the floor of the entryway before I stumble to my bed.

My bed.

The bed I'll no longer share with Matt.

The silent tears streaming down my face are the only visible signs of what just happened. As much as I resent them, I can't hold them back. I also can't fully comprehend Matt's betrayal.

I was so stupid.

Thankful that my mind and body are incapacitated by the flu, I don't let myself think about the canceled wedding or my uncertain housing options. Instead, I shut down my brain for a little while and get some sleep.

It's almost noon the next day when I finally crack open my eyes. My kidneys hurt like a bitch, and I actually stop to wonder if I'm forgetting about being punched a few times. And then I remember I was. I wasn't hit physically. But emotionally, I got my ass whooped last night.

One glance in the mirror confirms that I look as bad as I feel. I haven't had anything to eat or drink in too many hours to look remotely healthy. There are several alert notifications on my phone screen, but I don't bother to look at any of them. I'm not ready to face reality quite yet. I just need to take a little bit more time to feel better before I can fully embrace the next type of pain in my life.

The type of pain I never expected to feel and would never wish on my worst enemy.

The type of pain no one should feel.

The type of pain that comes from knowing the person you were about to devote your life to never really loved you at all.

CHAPTER SIX

TYLER

Her name is Britney, and her daughter is Harper. They stayed with Mom and me until almost nine thirty when her boyfriend finally showed up. The bass pounding out of the low-riding car shook the store windows so hard I was afraid they'd crack. Mom seemed hesitant to let Harper get inside that thing. She called out a warning about ear protection before they skidded off into the night.

As much as we tried to get her story, Britney wouldn't say much. She avoided all personal questions but at least she was willing to eat. Mom managed to get a full plate of pot roast in Britney while she fed Harper the soft potatoes and carrots.

Harper is two and a half but looks smaller than other two-year-olds I've seen. I don't know if it's malnourishment or just her genes, but she didn't seem as healthy as she should. Thunder rattles the window again before lightning cracks outside.

I hope they're both okay out there.

"Do you think she'll come back?" Mom has asked that every day since the two disappeared on us. It's been three days, and I'm not sure we'll ever see them again.

"I don't know, but I'm sure they're fine, Mom." I put my hand on her shoulder to stop her from pacing. "They've survived this long."

Mom shakes her head. "She said she graduated last spring. That's probably when they left her family. I don't know if they'll be able to survive a winter out there."

"She's not homeless. She said they stay nearby."

Mom raises an eyebrow and looks at me like I'm an idiot. "Don't you know that's code for homeless? Honey, she hadn't bathed in a long time. She's probably staying at the women's shelter on Ninth Street, but that place fills up. And it's certainly no place for a sweet baby to grow up."

"Do you want to go check on her or something?" I really hope that's not what she's suggesting. I don't want anything bad to happen to them either, but Mom doesn't need this kind of stress in her life.

"No, I'm sure they're alright." She's wringing her hands together, a sure sign of her anxiety over the situation. "But if she comes back, make sure we get them some food. Maybe I'll put together a little care package to keep up here, just in case."

"Care package? Those are my second favorite kind of packages." Chad steps up behind Mom and wraps his arm around her shoulder, winking at me.

"Oh, you." Mom laughs at his crude joke and swats at his arm. "You spend too much time cooped up in that firehouse."

"Yeah, probably." Chad drops the first three Rex Calloway paperbacks on the counter, and I have to keep myself from squealing in excitement. "But until I have someone waiting for me at home, it's the most lucrative way to spend my days."

Mom gives me a knowing look, as if trying to encourage me to take the bait and ask him out. *Sorry, Mom. Not gonna happen.*

I pick up volume one and hold it up. "You already have this, don't you?"

"Damn, you're good. Are you like the Rain Man of customer purchases?"

I feel my cheeks pink as I realize it is a little creepy that I know what books he has in his personal library. Of course, if he knew I was Rex Calloway, it probably wouldn't seem as stalkerish. "No, I just know you're following this series."

"Yeah, well, they aren't for me. I've got a buddy going through a rough time right now. He just canceled his engagement and is getting over the flu. I figured he might need something to keep him distracted."

"That's sweet." Mom reaches across the counter and picks up volume three. "This is my favorite. I really thought Jaxon was going to hook up with that professor at the end."

"Which one?" Chad and I ask at the same time.

There was a male professor and a female professor in that storyline. And since I haven't outed Jaxon in any of the books yet, I'm curious to know what she thinks.

"Well, I'm not sure." She shrugs and looks between us. "That's why I was so excited throughout that book. I just wanted him to find love."

I roll my eyes. Mom is such a romantic. I guess that's why it was so easy for me to come out to her. She didn't even really seem surprised when I told her I had a boyfriend in sixth grade. "Maybe in the next book."

"Fingers crossed." Mom puts the three books in a bag and slides it across the counter to Chad. "And I'm sure your friend will love these."

"Oh, Marge." Chad snaps his fingers. "Before I forget, I'm kind of in charge of finding businesses to host a Toys for Tots drive this year. Have you done that before?"

Mom shakes her head. "No, but I'm certainly willing to help."

"Great! Can we put a barrel in here to collect donations? Maybe it'll encourage people to buy books to donate."

My attraction to Chad grows a little more as I realize what a good guy he really is. He obviously cares about others in a way that a lot of single men his age don't, myself included. It's not that I don't care, I just don't go out of my way to help others like I probably should. The way he obviously does—on and off the job. Hell, the man was pushed off a building a few months ago while trying to save someone during a fire, and he still went back to work as soon as the doctors cleared him. That takes a hell of a lot more guts than I'll ever have.

"Of course." Mom looks excited by the prospect of hosting a drive. Truthfully, it does sound kind of fun. "And if there's anything else we can do to help, just let us know."

"Thanks, Marge. That means a lot." Chad runs his fingers through his hair and looks a little stressed. "We have a pretty huge goal this year, and it's gonna be tough to meet it. Last year, we fell short. No one wants that to happen again."

"You can count on us to do our part." Mom looks ready to salute Chad and maybe break into the national anthem.

Chad takes the bag with his books and steps back. "Well, I better get these delivered. Josh is probably a balled-up mess at this point."

"Does he like cookies?" Mom asks Chad out of nowhere.

Chad's eyes sparkle. "Probably. I know I definitely like cookies."

Mom holds up a finger. "Wait here. I'll be right back."

When she disappears out the back door, I feel a little guilty for being annoyed that Chad and his friend are going to get the batch of oatmeal chocolate chip cookies she baked last night.

But he's not only a good Samaritan and a freakin' fireman, he's also a good friend trying to help a buddy during a rough time.

Yeah, he definitely deserves the cookies more than I do.

CHAPTER SEVEN

JOSH

I think my flu has run its course, but it's hard to tell because my whole body still aches. Although, now I think it's from depression and not actual illness.

Matt has called a few times over the past two days, but I haven't picked up. Thankfully, he hasn't shown up at the house either. Technically, the lease is in his name so he has every right to come back and demand that I leave.

But I don't think he'll do that.

As much of a self-centered dick as he can be, he's a good guy when he wants to be. And I do think he loved me in some way. Obviously, not enough to be faithful to me, but I think he'll give me space to find a place of my own. As long as I don't wait too long to do it.

I consider taking a shower. I'll probably feel a little more human after, but it requires too much effort. I've hardly gotten out of bed at all over the past two days. Until I have to be back at work, I don't expect to move any farther than the bathroom, and occasionally, the kitchen.

I force myself up and go brush my teeth to get the top layer of fuzz off them. I'm about to crawl back into bed when I hear my doorbell. I tense in fear, wondering if I'm wrong about Matt giving me space. Maybe two days is long enough. Splashing some water on my face, I try to wake up.

Damn, I look like hell.

I run my wet fingers through my hair to tame the beast before stepping out into the living room. Chad's big head fills the glass window in my front door, and I crack a smile for the first time in days. He's such a dork.

I open the door and invite the goofball inside. "Hey, man. Good to see you."

"You too. Just wanted to make sure you're still alive." He walks in and takes a look around. "And you haven't even destroyed his house...so that's something."

I roll my eyes. "Nah, not my style. Actually, he gave notice to the landlord so I need to start looking for a new place anyway." Now that I'm feeling better, I'll make it a priority.

"Here. Brought you these." Chad hands me a paper bag.

I take a peek inside. "Books?"

"Yes, books. You know, people read them for entertainment."

I try not to frown. It was a thoughtful gift, just not something I'm usually into. "Oh, thanks." I don't know when I last read a book.

Chad claps me on the shoulder as he walks to the kitchen. "Trust me, you'll like them. You might even learn something."

"Oh, yeah?" I laugh and pull one of the copies out to read the back cover. "Do they teach you how to tell if your fiancé is cheating on you?"

The smile drops from Chad's face, and he walks back to me, pulling me in for a hug. "I'm sorry, man. I know that really sucks. He's a dick."

I just nod against Chad's shoulder. There's nothing else to say at this point.

After a long moment, Chad pulls back and leans against the counter. "Have you heard from him?"

I let out a deep breath. "No. He's tried calling, but I'm not answering. I have nothing to say to him."

"Good." Chad seems happy with my answer before he looks around the kitchen. "You got any food around here or should we go out to lunch?"

"Lunch?" I look at the clock on the microwave. "I just woke up."

"Fine. Brunch. Go get dressed."

~**~

Chad and I end up at a little taco stand downtown. It's one of my favorite places, but Matt hates it so it's been a while since I've been here.

"What about you?" I ask in between bites and after ignoring more questions about Matt.

"What about me?" Chad pops a chip loaded with guacamole into his mouth.

"How's your love life going? Anyone new in your bed?"

Chad snorts. "Nope, no one new because I don't have a love life. I have a fuck life...and there's nothing new to report on that front. Just the same fuck buddies I see now and then."

"Dude, you can't do that forever."

"Why not?" He looks at me like I'm an idiot. "It's fun, and I never have to worry about walking in on my boyfriend fucking someone else."

I could be upset by that comment, but I'm not. I know it's not his intention to hurt me. Instead, I raise an eyebrow and smirk. "Because you encourage everyone you're with to always bring a buddy?"

"Exactly! And now that you're single, maybe I'll fold you into the mix. There's a search and rescue dude I see now and then. He's fucking amazing...and an amazing fuck." Chad waggles his eyebrows. "Now you can see how the other half lives."

"Thanks, but I'll pass." Just the thought makes my stomach roll. Supposedly, most guys would kill for a three-way...but not me. I've never had any interest in sharing.

"You don't know what you're missing, man."

I shake my head. "Nope, one guy at a time for me. I'm old-school like that."

"That's not even old-school, dude. That's like Catholic school."

I choke and almost spit my burrito all over the place. "Hey, I've dated some Catholic school boys. Those dudes are freaky."

"Oh yeah?" Chad looks intrigued. "Maybe I need to go hang out near the Jesuit university. I can offer to do some CPR classes or something."

I laugh at his inappropriate suggestion. "You're disgusting."

"I'm not." Chad takes a moment to chew his taco so it doesn't all fly out at me while he talks. "I'm just content with my lot in life."

"Is that so?" I lean back in the chair and fold my arms over my chest. "And what exactly is your lot in life?"

"To be a stud, obviously." Chad holds his arms out as if displaying himself to the world. "And to bring joy to men up and down the Rockies."

"What about when all these men start to settle down and have families? Then what are you gonna do?"

Chad shrugs and his expression changes to something less cheery. "I don't know. Maybe I'll adopt."

"Seriously?" I was just joking around, but this looks like something he's given some thought to. "You want to have kids?"

Chad looks up at me, squinting against the sunlight streaming into his eyes. "I think I could do okay with a kid or two."

I smile at the sincerity in his voice. "Yeah, I think you could."

CHAPTER EIGHT

TYLER

"June just gave notice," Mom says, folding up a piece of paper and sliding it back in the envelope it came from.

"Really? When is she leaving?"

"End of the month." Mom looks personally offended that one of our best tenants has decided to move out.

"Damn." June has been renting the apartment above the store for the past year and a half and has been a dream. She pays on time, and we never hear a peep out of her. "Alright. I can put another ad on Craigslist and see what the market looks like."

"Thanks, honey. And can you also put a note on the bulletin board? I hate using Craigslist. Maybe one of our customers is looking for a place."

"Sure thing." The bulletin board at the front of the store usually has a few rental listings and cars for sale next to the standard pet sitting ads and coupons for the deli down the street.

During a quiet period at the store, I dig up our old Craigslist ad and make a few modifications, including bumping up the rent by $200 just to see if that'll hold. After a quick search of comparable apartment listings, it looks like rates have gone up, but we'll see if there's actually demand at that price.

I'm just about to hand over the till to Kim so I can head out for lunch when a gorgeous man walks in. He's never been in before because I would remember his brown hair with cute curls that turn up around his ears and the sexiest blue eyes I've ever seen. Damn, he's hot.

He walks a few feet inside and then just stops, frozen like a deer in headlights in the middle of the entryway. I give him a minute to get his bearings, but when he doesn't seem very comfortable, I clear my throat to get his attention.

"Excuse me, can I help you find something?"

"Oh, yeah." He startles and turns to me. As soon as our eyes lock, his shoulders relax, and he slowly smiles. "I think you can help. I'm looking for a couple books in the…" He pulls a piece of paper out of his back pocket and reads it to me. "It's called the Glass Bay series by Rex Calloway."

I bite my lip to keep from smiling too wide. "Uh-huh, I'm familiar with it."

"Oh, cool." He stuffs the paper in his pocket and takes a few steps closer to me. "Well, I have the first three books, and now I want to get the rest of them."

This time, I don't try to hide my smile as I walk around the back of the counter to guide him to my books. "That's great. It's a popular series."

"Yeah, I'm not usually much of a reader, but these just sucked me in. Now I need to know what happens next." The man almost seems embarrassed to admit that he likes a book. He must not have gotten the memo that nerd is the new jock.

"A good book will do that to you." I'm not usually one to brag, but since he'll never know that I'm Rex Calloway, I allow myself this brief moment of blatant self-promotion.

"Actually, my buddy loves the series and bought me a couple copies when I was sick. I guess I owe him one."

That jogs a memory, and I take a good look at the guy. He's wearing a Denver firefighters T-shirt. "You aren't talking about Chad, are you?"

"Sure am," he says with a big smile. "You know Chad?"

"He's a customer and mentioned buying books for a friend who wasn't feeling well last week."

"Yeah, we work together."

Of course you do. "He's a cool guy. He comes in at least once a week."

"He said the newest one is the best but that I should read them in order."

"Yeah, you have good timing. We just got the paperbacks a few days ago for the latest release, and we're almost out of stock." I point to the shelf lined with Rex Calloway books. "But we should have at least one copy of all the books you haven't read yet."

"Sick." He looks like a kid in a candy store. It's sexy as fuck. His blue eyes seem to twinkle as he picks up book four from the shelf and flips to the back cover.

I stick my hands in my pockets and try to find an excuse to hang around. Unfortunately, I can't think of one.

"Well, I'll be up front if you need help with anything else."

"Sure thing...uh, what was your name?"

"Tyler."

"Hey, Tyler." He holds out a large, strong hand to me. "I'm Josh."

And I'm your future husband.

~**~

Fucking hell, Josh is gorgeous. Do all the men at the fire station look like underwear models? If so, I think it's time for an inspection from the fire marshal.

I delay my lunch plans until Josh is ready to check out. As soon as his books are in a bag, I give him my best smile. "Is there is anything else you need from me?"

Please ask for my number.

Please ask for my number.

Josh just smiles and reaches for the bag. "No, that'll be it."

"Thanks and come again." I offer feebly as he walks out the door. Clearly, I'm not destined to be with a fireman.

I call out to Kim before I step away from the counter. "Leaving for lunch. It's all you."

"Gotcha. Have a good one." Kim is probably reading some trashy skin lit book in a dark corner somewhere.

Good for her.

~**~

On Sunday afternoon, Mom and I are both shocked when Britney and Harper walk inside the store. Mom has her care package ready to go with some lame excuse about her friend's granddaughter not needing the clothes and snacks anymore.

Britney tries to refuse the gifts, but Mom is insistent and eventually wins the battle. She has a knack for getting her way. I think that's partially my fault for always trying to keep her happy after Dad died.

Britney looks uncomfortable, but the way she's eying the Clif bars is an indicator that she's hungry. Those things are okay but definitely not drool-worthy.

"Um, we'll just be reading, if that's okay." Britney inches toward the children's section of the store with Harper closely following behind.

"Of course," Mom says. "Stay as long as you want. I was just about to make some sandwiches, so I'll be back in a few minutes with snacks."

"You don't have to do that." Britney's eyes are wide, and she glances at the door as if considering a run for it.

"I insist." Mom waves away her protests and disappears into the back of the store.

"Sorry." I smile at the girls, hoping to settle Britney's anxiety. "She doesn't take no for an answer very well."

"Yeah, I'm learning that." Britney laughs for the first time. She actually looks somewhat relaxed as she lowers her guard. "My mom was the same way so I understand."

I notice the past tense and know I shouldn't pry, but I ask anyway. "Does your mom live around here? She must love having a granddaughter to spoil."

Britney shakes her head and looks nervous again. "No, we don't talk much anymore. Um, we'll be reading." She quickly drags Harper away from my intrusive and unwelcome questions.

Mom returns twenty minutes later with a basket of sandwiches. "Mom, you're going to embarrass her and scare her away. I don't think she likes all the attention."

Her eyes go wide as she realizes that might be true. "Okay, I'm going to put this out for everybody. We'll call it a customer appreciation picnic." She quickly moves to a table closer to the children's section and clears the books off it. "Put these apple slices on a plate for Harper. We're going to feed those girls whether they like it or not."

~**~

Mom's little trick to get Britney and Harper fed actually worked out well for all of us. I print out a receipt of the days sales and hand it to my mom. "Looks like your little plan worked."

"Of course it did." She slides her glasses off the top of her head to read the small print.

"Up by twenty percent. Not too bad for a Sunday."

"See that," Mom blows on her nails then swipes them dramatically across her shoulder, "I'm not as old as you like to think. I've still got it."

I raise my hands up with palms out. "Hey, I never said you were old or that you didn't have *it*...whatever *it* is."

"Oh, you know what *it* is. *It* is brilliant in the idea department. I can still best any one of you young guys when it comes to great ideas."

"Okay..." That's random. I really have no idea what she's talking about at this point.

"And it just so happens I have another great idea."

"Oh god. I'm afraid to ask." This woman can never just take a win quietly.

"You don't have to ask because I'm going to tell you." She clears her throat dramatically, as if speaking in front of a crowd. "I think you should ask Chad out on a date."

"Mom... We've been through this before. He's not into me."

"How do you know that? He's always flirting with you, and he comes in all the time." If that's all that mattered, I'd be married to five different women who eye fuck me every time their cougar book club meets at the store.

"He's just a flirt by nature, but he hasn't responded when I flirt back. Trust me, there's nothing there."

She looks crestfallen at the reality that there won't be a firefighting son-in-law in her future. "Fine, but you really do need to start getting serious about settling down. I want grandchildren before I'm too old to enjoy them."

"Alright, enough with the guilt trip. I'm getting out there. And if I find someone, you'll be the first to know." That's total bullshit, but it shuts her up.

The fact is, I am getting out there. But only for one fuck at a time. I'm not actively looking for a serious relationship. I don't even give my number to most guys I'm with. But, I'm out there...and I'm always open to more. At least, in theory I am.

Chad and Josh must work the same schedule because a few hours after Chad stops in for magazines or new books, Josh always stops by. It's been two weeks since he picked up the rest of the Rex Calloway books but he came in a few days ago for a grilling cookbook.

Today, he wanders around the store for a while before heading toward me. I'm alphabetizing some self-help books that were reorganized. Apparently, someone didn't like the alphabetical system and arranged each book by size, smallest to largest. Then, for the books that were the same height, it appears they arranged by width.

"Hey, Ty. How's it going?"

"Good." I brush some dust off my cheek with my forearm. "Just workin'."

"Hey, I was hoping you could help me find some more Rex Calloway books. I just finished the last Glass Bay book and don't have anything to read until the next one comes out in a few weeks."

"Unfortunately, there aren't any more." God, why can't I write faster? I'd give anything to remove the disappointed look from Josh's face. "But I can recommend a few others in the same genre that I think you'll enjoy."

"Yeah, that'd be great. Um, when you're done." He gestures to the mess of books piled around me.

"Actually, these can wait. Darren will be in soon. He loves to alphabetize."

Josh laughs as I neatly pile the stacks of books left to be shelved and lead him two aisles over to the suspense thriller section.

"These two series are both really good. They actually inspired me to wr—start reading the Rex Calloway books."

Holy shit. I almost outed myself for the first time ever. I bend down and pull out the first few books in the series I think he'll like most.

"Here, try these." It could just be wishful thinking, but I swear I can feel Josh checking out my ass. But he's human. Just because he checks me out doesn't mean he's interested in anything else.

"Great. I'll take 'em." His blue eyes look so sexy when he smiles. Especially when the smile is directed at me.

I clear my throat and square my shoulders. "Great. Let's get you checked out."

~**~

When Josh seems to be hanging around after his books are paid for, I decide to try my luck and ask him out, once and for all. This way, at least I know I tried.

"Hey, Josh."

"Hmm?"

"Do you want to get coffee sometime?"

He looks a little confused before it sinks in that I'm asking him out. "Uh, well... Actually, I just ended a serious relationship so...you know."

"You don't drink coffee anymore?" I grin to let him know I'm not trying to be bitchy.

"Well, yeah I do. I just... Um, coffee sounds great, but I'm not ready for more than that."

God, he's adorable.

"Okay." I smile in the least intimidating way I can manage. "Coffee without sex. Is that what you're saying?"

Josh coughs and his cheeks pink up just a bit. "Yeah, I think that's what I'm saying."

"Okay, I can handle that." I laugh as he backs away from the counter.

"So, when?"

Ooh, he's eager? That's a good sign.

I lift my phone to check the time. "I usually take a break between three and six. Are you free today?"

"Yeah, I can come back here at around three."

"Excellent." I head back to the stack of books I left on the floor. I wasn't actually going to make Darren work them. That's just cruel. "I'll see you then for our 'not a date,'" I say cheerily as he walks out the door.

When Thunder Rolls

CHAPTER NINE

JOSH

Coffee without sex. God, could I be any lamer? But I panicked. I didn't expect him to just ask me out in the middle of the bookstore. But he did, and I agreed.

By the time I get home, I definitely need a nap. Or maybe a run. Suddenly, I feel a burst of pent-up energy. What was I thinking? Am I seriously going to have coffee with the guy from the bookstore?

Not just a guy.

Tyler. With that sexy blond hair that falls over his eyes when he's looking down and those almost clear irises that are always watching me. And he is always watching me. I didn't notice it at first, but it's become apparent that he's interested.

I might have been interested too if Chad hadn't made it abundantly clear that Tyler is all about quick hookups. I'm definitely not ready for real dating, and no way can I just hook up with someone. Especially someone I actually like. That's just not me.

Hell, I haven't even moved out of Matt's house yet, and I'm already going on a date. But this isn't a date. It's just me and a friend having a cup of coffee.

At least, that's what I tell myself as I'm flipping through the clothes in my closet. As promised, I packed up all of Matt's shit and rented a storage unit for him for the next thirty days. I just couldn't stomach looking at his stuff anymore.

But he has a much better wardrobe than I do. I almost regret packing up everything because I could use some of his froufrou jeans right about now.

Since I made such a big deal about this not being a date, I go to the opposite extreme and decide on messy casual. An old pair of old jeans and a Nike T-shirt that I usually wear to the gym is perfect for coffee. And it definitely screams "no sex expected" to anyone with eyeballs.

Since I am too amped up to nap, I get online and start looking for rentals. A few of the guys at the station have offered to let me stay on their couch or guest bed for a little while. And while I appreciate the offers, I don't want to do that if I can avoid it. I am a grown-ass man, and I should have my own place. I'm too old to couch surf like a teenager.

I'm surprised by the number of one-bedroom apartments and studios available near the station. I was afraid I'd end up on the other side of town and would get stuck in traffic going to and from work.

In the spirit of efficiency, I write out a generic inquiry note and start sending it to all the property managers with decent listings. Hopefully a few of the good ones are still available.

I'm just about to shut down my laptop when one listing in particular gets my attention.

One bedroom, one bath above small bookstore. Private entrance, kitchenette, no pets. Email Tyler for an appointment.

Well, shit. This seems like more than a coincidence. I consider sending him the generic email but decide against it. I'll wait until this afternoon and bring it up over coffee.

Who knows, maybe he and I were meant to be friends after all.

~**~

I walk into the store at exactly three. Tyler's bright smile greets me and instantly causes a beaming smile of my own. He really is a damn good-looking man.

"Hey, Josh." He motions to another guy on the other side of the store then steps away from the counter. "I'm just about done here."

"Great." I link my fingers together and hold them in front of my pelvis, not really sure what to do with my hands. I feel extremely awkward picking him up for our non-date. I haven't done the dating thing in a long time. When I met Matt, we moved in together almost immediately because he needed help with the rent. And before that, I was in a long-term relationship with my college boyfriend so I never really did the "meeting friends and roommates" thing. "I'm ready when you are."

~**~

I try to pay for my own coffee and blueberry muffin, but Tyler insists on paying since he asked me to come. Knowing he probably doesn't make a lot working at a small bookstore makes me feel a little guilty, but it's only a few dollars.

Once we both have our orders, we settle into a couple of wingback chairs in the corner. Definitely not too intimate, which allows me to fully relax.

"So you're feeling better?" Tyler peeks at me from under his long blond lashes as he blows on his steaming coffee.

"What do you mean?" Could he tell how nervous I was earlier?

"Chad said you were sick a few weeks ago. You know, when he bought the books. Obviously, you're fine now."

"Oh, right. Yeah, it was just the flu." And a broken heart. Although, that's not something I want to talk about with Tyler.

"That's good. I hate being sick." He sticks his tongue out in an adorable expression. "I love food too much. When I lose my appetite, I get really cranky."

I chuckle at his honesty before taking a sip of my coffee. "Yeah, I think I lost a few pounds that week."

Tyler lets his eyes roam up and down my body. "Lost or found, your body is doing just fine."

Okay, now I full-on laugh. "I've never heard that one before."

Tyler laughs. "I like to make up cheesy lines as I go. But I'm not that creative so they're usually pretty bad. Just wait, you'll hear some doozies if you spend enough time with me."

Why does that sound so appealing?

"Oh, hey." I put my muffin down and lean forward so I'm talking closer to Tyler. "I was looking through the apartment listings online and found one located above a bookstore. You wouldn't happen to have an apartment for rent, would you?"

Tyler's eyes light up. "We do! You looking to move?"

I shrug. "Yeah, the lease is up on my place in a few weeks. I'm trying to get out as soon as possible."

"Well, the current tenant is moving out at the end of the month, if you're really interested. Is that soon enough?"

"That's perfect. I'm definitely interested." As soon as I realize the double meaning of my words, I turn away and focus on my muffin, hoping he doesn't see my cheeks blush.

"Mom will be thrilled." Tyler is watching me again. And as much as I want to pretend there isn't lust in his eyes, I can't keep myself from watching him back. Wondering what those full lips would feel like against mine. Imagining them kissing down my chest until they reached my cock.

Fuck, what am I doing? These jeans aren't made for hiding a hard-on, and I definitely don't want Tyler to notice I'm thinking about him in a physical way. I'm not ready for anything yet. It's only been a few weeks since Matt and I canceled our damn engagement. I'm months, maybe years, away from seeing other men in a sexual way... At least, I should be, right?

~**~

We end up staying at Starbucks much longer than I expected. In fact, I'm actually disappointed when Tyler realizes it's after six, and he needs to get back to the store. When he stands up to leave, I stand too, not sure what I should do next.

Does he expect me to walk him back? Should I shake his hand? Is this a hugging situation?

He must be able to read my indecision because he pulls me in for a hug and holds me for a few moments. "Let me know when you want to check out the apartment."

I nod against his shoulder, happy to be held by someone.

"And maybe we can have coffee again?"

"Next time is my treat." I squeeze a little harder before Tyler pulls away.

"It's *not* a date!" Tyler teases and winks at me before he disappears out the front door. I just stand there dumbly in the middle of Starbucks, watching him go.

Damn, he has a fine ass.

CHAPTER TEN

TYLER

An entire week later, Josh still hasn't made it back into the store. He said he's interested but June was home sick when Josh wanted to see the place. And then he went back to work for a four-day shift. I'm beginning to worry he's decided against the apartment, but I'm holding out hope and have deleted the online listing. The flyer is still tacked to the bulletin board, but I've deterred the few people who have asked about it.

It's inventory time, and as the owner's son, I get the primary responsibility for the job. Kim and Darren take on some of the counting, but it's so tedious that Mom feels bad making them do it. Of course, she has no qualms about making her only son suffer through the monotony of counting thousands of books.

I'm deep in the weeds of the historical fiction section when a familiar voice falls over me like a caress. A shiver runs down my spine as I imagine Josh calling my name in other situations.

Naked situations.

"Hey, Tyler." I look up and try not to stare at his crotch...which is right at my eye level. "Do you think your tenant would mind if I took a look at the apartment today?"

Oh right. He's not here to see me. Obviously.

"Not at all." Of course, Mom has pretty much decided he's the ideal tenant. If Josh likes the place, it's his. God, I hope he likes the place. "June has most of her stuff boxed up and knows we're showing it. We can go up anytime."

"Great." He rocks forward and back on his heels with an uncertain look on his face. "Um, when do you think you might have a few minutes?"

Oh, duh. He means now. "I just need to finish this row, and then I'll grab her key from the house. Give me five minutes."

~**~

"It's not much." I sweep my hand across the open living room/dining room area. "But it's not bad for one person."

"Looks great." Josh toes his shoes off at the door and follows me in. I forgot that June doesn't wear shoes indoors...but she's leaving in a few days so she can deal with a little dirt tracked in. "And utilities are included?"

"Yeah, water, power and Wi-Fi are all included since the bookstore pays for those. But if you want cable or a landline, you'll need to have those turned on. The wiring is already in place so you just need to make the calls."

"Sweet." Josh peeks through the open bedroom door. "Can I look in here?"

"Of course." I follow him to the doorway but don't go inside the room. This could be Josh's bedroom someday, and it feels intrusive for me to just let myself in right now. Besides, there isn't much to see. It's just a simple square room and a wall closet. Nothing special. "This is all June's furniture, but if you don't have your own, we have a spare bedroom set in the garage."

"No, that's fine. I have my own stuff." Josh walks to the window and looks out at the house Mom and I share. "Is that where you live?"

I press my chest against the doorway and nod. "Yup. I moved back in with Mom awhile back to help her out. And so she could get the rental income from this place."

"That's nice." Josh smiles and stares at me from across the room. "It's great that you're willing to help her out. Not everyone would do that."

"Eh." I shrug and push off the wall when Josh approaches the door. "I like hanging out with her. And she's a great cook."

"Mmm." Josh moans and pats his belly. "Speaking of food, have you eaten?"

"No, not since breakfast."

He checks his watch. "It's after two. Aren't you hungry?"

"Now that you're reminding me, yeah. I'm starving."

"Me too. You wanna grab a pizza?"

Is he asking me on a date? No, definitely not. "Sure. Sounds good."

After I lock up the apartment, we head into the store to tell Mom and Kim that I'm leaving for lunch. Mom is almost bouncing on her toes when she sees Josh with me.

"So, what do you think?" Her hands are folded in front of her chest like she's praying for the right answer.

"About the apartment?" When she nods, Josh chuckles. "I love it. It's great."

"Oh, wonderful." She leaps forward and into his arms, startling him with a big hug. "I'm so glad. You're perfect."

Josh laughs harder. "Wow, thanks. I don't hear that nearly enough."

I make a mental note to tell him he's perfect.

Often.

Because he sure as hell is.

~**~

Josh is officially moving in on October first.

I couldn't be more excited. He's still standoffish whenever I flirt with him, but I catch him checking me out often enough to know I might have a chance with him.

Someday.

Definitely not anytime soon, though. And that's part of the reason why I don't understand my own hesitance when Baker, a guy I see now and then, calls me up to have a drink.

Any other time that I've heard from Baker has always been good news. He's hot and a good lay, so there's no reason for me not to be excited to see him. But in the back of my mind, I feel like I shouldn't—like I shouldn't see anybody.

It doesn't make any sense because Josh is barely a month out of his engagement. It'll probably be several more before he'll consider anything beyond having coffee or lunch with me. And I obviously can't wait around forever for a lunch date.

After a few moments of contemplation, I respond to Baker and tell him I'll meet him at the Unicorn at ten. It's been over a month since I've been out, and that's way too long.

When Thunder Rolls

Chapter Eleven

Josh

"Thanks for stopping by, man." I open the door wider and let Chad inside the house first. "But I'm pretty much packed up. There's not really a lot to do."

Chad, Jet, and Cooper all give me the same indulgent smirk. "We're not here to help you pack, idiot." Chad walks straight to the kitchen and pulls a beer from the fridge. "We're here to take you out."

"Out where? It's almost nine o'clock." There's nowhere I want to go that's even open at nine o'clock.

"Out, man. You know...the bar. I know it's been a while, but that's the place where friends get together and have a drink and dance, and if they're lucky, they get lucky."

I chuckle and shake my head. "Oh, no, no, no. Thanks, but I don't think so. That's a nice offer, but I'm not a club type of person. I was just about to take a shower and climb into bed."

Chad turns to Jet. "Told you it was bad. We should've been here weeks ago."

Jet looks a little horrified. "I had no idea."

I turn to Cooper, hoping he can be the voice of reason. He's been sober for over a year and doesn't need to go to a bar. Hopefully, he can talk them out of this nonsense. "Come on, man. You're not going to make me do this, are you?"

Cooper just shrugs. "It's not my idea. These two seem to think you're going to start collecting cats if we don't get you out of here immediately."

Turning back to Chad, I give him my best puppy dog eyes. "I promise not to get any cats. I just really don't want to go out tonight."

"Too bad." He brushes past me, shoving his beer into my hand as he does. "I'll go find you something to wear."

Oooh, I have him there. "That might be a problem. I've only left out gym clothes and what I need for work. Everything else is packed. You know I'm moving in a couple days, right?"

Chad stares into my closet with a look of horror on his face. "Dear god, you're serious." He turns to me. "How can you not have any decent clothes?'

I laugh for the first time all day. "I was engaged. It's not like we were going clubbing on a regular basis."

Chad mumbles something, and I swear the words "no wonder" and "he left" are part of his little rant, but I don't call him out on it.

"You must have some other clothes in this house somewhere. Otherwise, we have to go back to my place so I can dress you."

Chad only wears clothes two sizes too small for him, and I've got a good twenty pounds on him, so that is definitely not an option. "Sorry. I guess I can't go out tonight. The only other clothes around are the bags of shit I'm donating to Goodwill."

Chad raises an eyebrow. "Where're these bags?"

"You're not gonna find anything in there." I point to a few garbage bags on the floor. "That stuff either doesn't fit me or is ugly as fuck."

Chad gives me an evil smirk. "Perfect! I'm sure we'll find something."

Unfortunately, he does. Chad seems very proud of himself when he discovers a black performance shirt that I stopped wearing a couple years ago because it was too tight around my chest and a pair of Matt's jeans that were mixed in with mine when I packed up his clothes.

I hold up the jeans and shake my head. "No way in hell these things are going to fit me."

"Put them on," Chad says, rolling his finger in the air to get me to speed it up. "We don't have all day."

As predicted, I can't get them past my thighs. I give Chad a smirk of my own. "Oh well, I guess you guys will have to go without me."

Chad narrows his eyes and unbuttons his own jeans, tearing them off his body before I have a chance to look away. Of course, he's not wearing anything underneath so I'm left staring at his thick cock in the middle of my bedroom.

"What are you doing?" My heart is about to beat out of my chest. Is he planning to fuck me right here if I'm not willing to go out to the bar to get laid tonight?

Chad wads up his jeans and throws them across the room at me. "Put these on and give me those."

"What?"

"You heard me. Put on my jeans, and I'll wear those. My thighs are little smaller, so they should fit me okay. And my jeans were a little loose. You'll get into them."

I hold up his jeans with two fingers. "Dude, these have your ball sweat all over them." I'm not about to put them on. No way, no how.

"Well, if you had any decent clothes in this house, you wouldn't have to. You're wearing underwear, so don't worry about it. Just put them on so we can get going. You're making everybody wait."

Damn him for invoking my need for never inconveniencing other people. "Fine." I shimmy out of the tight jeans and kick them to Chad so he can cover up that monster of his. Then I squeeze into his jeans, barely able to breathe once they're all the way up.

They're two sizes too small, but at least I can get the zipper up. "You know I'm not going to be able to sit down tonight, right?"

Chad laughs as he checks out his ass in the mirror. "You don't need to sit down. You need to dance and be able to lean against a wall while someone else takes care of you."

"Whatever." I don't bother trying to argue with him anymore. At this point, I just want to get this night over with.

"Put on some cologne, and we'll get out of here." Chad turns to check out his back side in the full-length mirror. "Oh, and I'm keeping these jeans. My ass looks amazing in them."

He's not wrong about that.

When Thunder Rolls

CHAPTER TWELVE

TYLER

The Unicorn is packed when I arrive. I'm surprised because it usually doesn't get busy until later. But there's an indie band playing tonight, so it's standing room only. Some people shy away from crowds, but I actually prefer the anonymity that comes with being lost in the crowd. I have a reputation for being overly flirty in situations like this, and I don't mind that reputation.

There's a certain liberation that comes with being able to let go of all inhibitions and just be wild for a few hours. I'm always safe and don't usually get too drunk, so it's a fun way for me to let loose now and then. I scan the room for Baker but don't see him. He isn't usually late but he's a busy guy who tends to overbook. Just to make sure he's still planning to show, I open my phone and shoot him a quick text.

Getting a drink from the bar. Text when you arrive.

Running late. Be there in 10.

Trixie sees me approaching the bar and immediately points to a bottle of Cîroc. She knows my usual, so I just raise an eyebrow and nod, knowing it'll be ready by the time I actually push through this crowd.

"Hey, girl, how are you doing?" I step around the end of the bar and give her a kiss on the cheek. "You're looking as gorgeous as ever."

"Thanks, sweetie. It's been a while since you've been in here. Everything okay with you?" She slides my drink over to me.

"I've been good. Just busy with Mom's store. It's inventory time, you know."

Trixie laughs. "God, I hate inventory here. I can't even imagine what it would be like in a bookstore."

"It sucks... Let me tell you." I reach for my wallet then change my mind. "You know what? I think we're going to put this on Baker's tab tonight."

Trixie nods and takes a look around the bar. "Is he even here? I haven't seen him."

"Not yet. He's running late but will be here in a few minutes."

"Good enough. You let me know if you need anything else." Trixie blows me a kiss before turning away to help other customers.

I lean an elbow against the end of the bar and take a sip of my ruby apple. It's delicious. Despite the clichés, I really love fruity drinks. And if I get sick, they taste much better coming up than the hard shit.

It's hard to see faces in the dim light, but from the corner of my eye, I catch a glimpse of Chad sitting at one of the tables. I take a moment to appreciate how good he looks before I realize who's sitting next to him. My mouth goes dry when I see Josh laughing at something Chad just said.

Josh is wearing a tight black shirt that outlines every muscle in his chest and shoulders. And his hair looks different...like he's gelled it in a different way. I know I'm staring, but I can't look away from his lips as they move when he talks. He seems to be having a really good time. His eyes almost sparkle when he laughs. I want to walk over to them to say hello, but I don't want to intrude on their evening.

I almost have the courage to push off the bar and walk over to their table when Josh's eyes meet mine. They're almost burning into me from across the room. I can't do anything but stare back. Even with twenty feet between us, I can feel his presence surrounding me. I can't see who else is at their table, but he's clearly having a good time.

It's not my place to intrude. I'm definitely not going to approach him. Instead, I force a smile and wave from where I'm standing.

Josh looks different now too. He's almost shy as he flicks his wrist in my direction like he's tipping his hat. It's a sweet and dorky gesture, and my smile just grows broader.

"Hey, beautiful." Baker's hand slides across my back and grips my hip as he steps against me. "Sorry I'm late. I wanted to look good for you."

I tear my eyes away from Josh and take a look at Baker. "Well, let's see how you did." I lean back, allowing my eyes to inspect every inch of his body. Erik Baker is tall and thin. At 6'3" and probably a hundred and eighty pounds of lean muscle, he's an impressive sight. He has some fancy job and always looks like he's coming from a board meeting. But he wears it well. "You're a little overdressed for me, but I like it."

Baker winks. "Just making it more fun when you undress me."

A part of me wants to turn back and look at Josh. But a bigger part of me is afraid of what I might see. Will he be making out with Chad? Will he give me an indication that he wants me to ditch Baker and go home with him?

No.

Either way, I don't want to see him right now. I'm here to be with Baker. He can give me what I need for the short-term. And I'll just have to continue working on Josh for the long-term.

I take a sip from my glass without breaking eye contact with Baker. "By the way, thanks for the drink you just bought me." I hold up my glass. "If you want one too, you should get one now. I'm not in the mood to wait around all night." Baker's fingers tighten around my hip, and he pulls me flush against his chest. "Fuck, I've missed you, Ty."

"Well, why don't you show me how much?"

~**~

Baker always has a car waiting outside the club. Usually, he comes in a limo, so we won't have to go far. Which is good because I don't want to be out all night. I've just started writing my next book, and I kind of want to get back to it.

But I really need this release. Jacking off to porn is only fun for so long. After a while, it's just sad. So when Baker drags me through the club, I keep my eyes straight ahead, making sure they don't stray to Chad or Josh as I pass right by their table.

The limo is waiting just outside the front door, and the driver quickly ushers us in before rushing around the front to get inside too. As soon as the door is closed behind us, Baker pulls me onto his lap, crushing his mouth against mine. Kissing is fine, but I don't have time for a lot of foreplay. I shift so my dick is pressing up against Baker's. Both shafts are hard and desperate for attention.

"Someone in a hurry?" Baker asks, sliding my hips forward and back a few inches so I'm skating over his dick.

"Uh huh. I want you. Enough wasting time." I unzip Baker's slacks, not even bothering with the belt or button. It takes a little bit of maneuvering to get him out of his silk briefs, but within seconds, his hard cock is pointing straight up at me and waiting for attention.

Wrapping my left palm around his shaft, I work him up and down while I get my jeans down past my knees. I don't want to bother with my ankle boots, so I just ease my pants as far down as they'll go then plant my knees on either side of Baker's thighs.

"We doing this?" I ask as I stroke him a little faster.

His head is thrown back against the seat, and his eyes are closed. "Mmm. Yes, we're definitely doing this." He reaches into his coat pocket and pulls out a strip of condoms and a couple packets of lube. "Here you go."

Baker is used to being taken care of. He doesn't do a lot of the heavy lifting when it comes to our hookups. That works out well since I'm more of a power bottom, topping without ever being on top.

It only takes me a minute to work some lube inside myself and get the condom on Baker. His dick is a little on the skinny side, but it's long enough to do the trick. Especially when I'm in control and know exactly how I need him. As soon as we're both ready, I lift up enough to position his tip at my opening.

It's been almost two months since I've had anyone inside me, so I drop down slowly, allowing him to push past my muscle before stopping to get used to the fullness. It only takes me a few seconds before I'm ready for more. Exhaling slowly, I lower myself until I'm a fully seated against Baker's thighs.

"Fuck, Ty. You feel so good. You're always so tight for me, baby."

I grunt in response and start bouncing up and down on his dick, riding him hard and fast to get what I want. Or rather, to get what I need.

"Baby, you need to slow down." Baker's palms tighten around my hips as he tries to slow me down, holding me above him so he doesn't shoot too quickly. Baker's only in his forties, but I think the stress of his job has removed at least fifteen or twenty years of his stamina, because he's usually done in just a few minutes. That sucked the first few times we were together. But now that I know I have to move quickly, I can usually beat him to completion.

It's almost become a game for me to come as quickly as possible when I'm with him. I curl my body away from Baker, almost creating a C-shape, so every time he thrusts inside me, he pounds right against my prostate.

It's an intense way to come, fast and hard without any gentle touches. But it works every time.

Just as Baker's face scrunches up and he clenches his jaw, I allow myself to let go and shoot my load all over the front of his fancy suit. Baker's fingers dig into my hips hard enough that I know they'll leave bruises. With a grunt, he arches up off the seat and pushes his cock as deep inside me as he can get while he rides out his own orgasm.

I feel a tiny bit of remorse for ruining his shirt and coat —but not much. If I know Baker, he'll probably jack off to those come stains for a week before tossing them out.

CHAPTER THIRTEEN

JOSH

It's not until I'm laughing and truly relaxing that I realize how much more fun it is to be out without Matt than it ever was to be out with him. He could be a dick sometimes and always had to have his way. Whenever we were out with friends, he tried to one-up everybody with better stories or more impressive accomplishments. I usually ended up having to apologize for him at the end of the night.

I think that's why we stopped going out. It just wasn't fun anymore. But watching Jet and Coop laugh at each other's jokes and cuddle against each other reminds me of what I was missing. I can finally say that I'm glad things didn't work out with Matt. I don't think I ever would've been as happy with him as these guys are together.

And I want to be that happy. I want to have what they have.

And although I don't want my mind to wander in that direction, I can't stop myself from thinking about what Tyler is doing with that stiff. Ty's so fun and playful, and seeing him with a businessman in a stuffy suit just doesn't make a lot of sense to me.

But it's not my business. I'm not interested in anything right now and certainly not with a player like Tyler. He's young and beautiful. He deserves to play the field with every hot guy he comes across.

He's hinted at being interested in me, but I quickly squashed that idea. I have no right to be bothered by the fact that he's with someone else tonight. Hell, he's probably with someone else every night. A low groan escapes my throat, causing Chad to turn to me. "What's wrong?"

"Nothing." I take a drink of my beer to avoid making eye contact with him.

Chad smirks and nudges Jet's hand to get his attention. "Oh, are you sad that Tyler is with Baker instead of coming over to talk to you?"

Jet nods from across the table. "Tyler, huh? He's a doll. And generally, a good tipper."

Cooper growls and turns to Jet. "Is he now?"

Jet smiles wide and leans against his partner's chest, giving him a soothing pat. "Yes, baby, for drinks. Nothing else."

Cooper raises a possessive eyebrow. "Never anything else?"

Jet's smile fades, and he looks stern. "I thought we weren't going to talk about our pasts anymore."

Cooper takes a deep breath then slowly nods. "Fine. I just wish you didn't have so many things to not talk about."

Jet closes his teeth around Cooper's earlobe and tugs down gently before whispering, "You're the only one I'll be talking about for the rest of my life. Isn't that good enough?"

Cooper turns to Jet, and any insecurity he might have been feeling seems to evaporate. "It's more than I'll ever deserve."

I turn away from the happy couple, giving them a moment of privacy for this intimate exchange. As fascinated as I am by watching them, it just makes me feel even worse about myself.

What a waste of two years of my life. I should've been looking for somebody who would love me the way Jet and Cooper love each other. Instead, I was letting Matt walk all over me, working my ass off while he was probably plowing into someone else's every night I was at work. I scoot my chair back and turn to Chad. "I think I'm gonna head out, man."

"Already?" Chad looks at his phone. "It's not even eleven. And you're supposed to be getting some tail while we're here."

I laugh at the absurdity of that. "You and I both know that was never going to happen."

Chad gives me a crooked smile and punches my shoulder. "Yeah, I knew it, but a guy can hope, right?"

I gesture to the packed dance floor. "Well, now you can go get your own tail without me weighing you down."

"You gonna get home okay?"

"Yep. I've got an Uber coming in..." I check my phone. "Two minutes. I'll catch you later."

Right as I step out into the cool night air, a limo pulls up in front of me and double parks. I wonder if it's a celebrity or just a bachelorette party coming to ogle the hot guys.

Unfortunately, I'm wrong on both counts. I feel sick to my stomach when the driver opens the back door, and Tyler steps out, tucking the front of his shirt back into his jeans as he waves goodbye to the man in the backseat.

I don't know what to say when he finally looks up and makes eye contact with me. Tyler's eyes go wide, but he recovers faster than I do and smiles casually. "Hey, Josh, good to see you."

"Yeah, you too." I watch the limo as it pulls away.

"Where's Chad?" Tyler looks behind me, apparently expecting to see Chad hiding there.

I shake my head to help myself focus. "Oh, he's still inside, but I was ready to call it a night."

Tyler cocks his head and looks confused. "But didn't you guys come together?"

I laugh and shake my head. "God, no. Not like that. He did pick me up, but only because he was forcing me to come out tonight instead of sitting around at home."

"Oh, do you need a ride?" Tyler asks, pulling his keys from his pocket.

God, he's sweet. "No, thanks. I've got an—" The gray Camry I'm expecting pulls up right in front of us. "That's me. I'll see you in a few days."

"Okay. See ya."

I watch him standing there as we pull away, and I can't help but wonder how different things will be when I'm living next door to Tyler. There are so many ways this can go.

Really well...or really bad.

Chapter Fourteen

Tyler

The last five days have dragged by as I've waited for today to come. Josh will finally be moving in. I know it's silly, and I shouldn't be so excited for him to be living just a few feet from my house, but I am. Even if nothing ever happens between us physically, he's a cool guy to hang out with.

I don't have a lot of guy friends. In fact, other than Kim and Darren at the store, I don't really have a lot of friends at all. I have some acquaintances, customers that I'm friendly with, and my list of regular hookups. But there isn't really anybody I would call to go watch a movie with or to grab dinner with except Josh. He's the first person who's been interested in spending time with me when sex was completely off the table.

It's nice.

Although, I hope sex isn't off the table forever. But even if it is, I'll be okay with that.

And despite my better judgment, I let myself fantasize about poker nights at his place and maybe getting together to watch movies on his off nights. That is, of course, on the nights when he's not out with Chad at a bar. That whole night still rubs me the wrong way. I shouldn't feel hurt by the fact that hanging out with me is coffee or pizza, but hanging out with Chad is beers and dancing.

But it doesn't matter.

I'll take what I can get. For now.

I'm just heading out the door to grab a sandwich when Josh almost walks right into me. He's hidden behind two large cardboard boxes, but I'd recognize that body anywhere. "Oh. Hi, Josh."

"Hey, Tyler." He stumbles backward to avoid me and bounces off the boxes Chad's carrying.

"Dude, watch it or all your shit is gonna end up scattered across the sidewalk."

"Sorry." Josh turns to Chad before looking back at me. "Sorry. I probably should've called to let you know we were coming, but Chad offered to help move some stuff in his truck, so I figured I should take advantage of the free labor."

Chad clears his throat from behind the boxes. "Uh, hate to break it to you, champ, but this labor ain't free. You're buying me lunch afterward. An expensive lunch."

Josh ignores Chad. "Anyway, is it okay for me to start taking stuff up?"

"Of course." I hold the door for them as they maneuver the boxes inside. "Let me go grab the keys, and I'll meet you out back."

Once I give Josh his set of keys, I hang around for a minute and offer to help bring stuff up. Josh and Chad both tell me not to worry about it. Although I don't feel like they're trying to get rid of me, I know they definitely aren't asking me to stay. So, I bow out and head to the deli to grab lunch.

By the time I get back, Chad's truck is gone, and I wonder if they're done unpacking. My question is answered an hour later when the truck is back and full of furniture.

I'm tempted to offer to help again, but they're big and muscular fireman. They don't need help from skinny little me to get a mattress and some tables up one flight of stairs.

It's almost four o'clock when Chad and Josh walk through the front door of the bookstore. "Hey, Tyler, you hungry?" Josh asks.

Chad puts his arm around Josh's shoulder. "Yeah. The big guy's buying lunch or," he looks at his watch, "I guess it's kind of an early bird dinner. You should come with us."

"Thanks, but I grabbed a sandwich a couple hours ago."

Josh's eyes look disappointed for just a second, but my attention quickly moves to Chad as he steps forward and reaches for my hand. "Oh, come on. You've got to come with us. This cheap ass never pays, so I want to make sure he gets stuck with a fat bill... And I can only eat so much by myself."

I laugh as I think about the few times Josh and I have been out. He's always offered to pay, even when I wouldn't let him. "Well..." I'm trying to think of an excuse for why I can't make it when Mom steps behind the counter and gives me a shove.

"You go on, honey. We're fine here. Don't you worry about us, okay?"

"Sure. Thanks, Mom." I look to the guys. "Should I change or..."

Josh shakes his head. "You look great."

My gaze locks on Josh's, and I can feel my heart beating faster as that smile cuts right through me. I know it's just a friendly smile that he gives everybody, but when he directs it my way, I feel ten feet tall.

Chad whistles loudly, and we all turn in his direction. "Dang, Marg, what have you been doing to get all these donations so early?" Chad tilts the barrel on one side to take a look at all the contents. "Are you threatening your customers if they don't leave a toy?"

Mom laughs, but it's not that far from the truth. She has been laying the guilt on pretty thick. "Well, some of us just have a natural charm that people can't say no to."

I snort out a laugh. "I can testify to that. This woman could sell ice to an Eskimo."

Josh's eyes never stray from my face as he reaches out to me. "Well, if you're ready, we can get going."

Chad pipes in. "I'll send someone from the station down to swap out your barrel this week so this one isn't overflowing."

"Thanks, sweetie. My sob story works a lot better when the barrel is empty than when it's stuffed with toys."

CHAPTER FIFTEEN

JOSH

I'm relieved when Chad insists that Tyler come with us to lunch. I didn't have the balls to beg, but I was looking forward to hanging out with him. Things have been crazy at work, and I've had to put in some overtime to cover for guys who are sick. But now that I'm fully out of Matt's house and on my own, I feel like I can start fresh. A new life in a new place...and maybe with a new friend.

Is that what Tyler is to me? Yeah, he's definitely a friend. But why does my stomach feel funny when I think of him? It's not the same kind of feeling I get when I think of Chad or any of the other guys I spend time with. There's something special about Ty that makes me think maybe I'm supposed to be here. Living where he lives and works.

Who knows? Maybe in time, there will be more to our friendship. Who am I kidding? I throw my head back and look up at the ceiling in my new apartment. I'm being stupid. Tyler isn't looking for more. He likes to pick up guys for a fast fuck, and then he goes out to find someone else.

I'm not judging him for it, but that's who he is. And that will never be someone for me. Not after what Matt did. I won't ever let myself be used in that way again. No, Tyler and I are meant to be friends. He can continue his booty calls, and I'll eventually get to the point of being ready to date someone looking for a serious relationship.

I hope.

~**~

It's almost eleven, and I've just turned off the lights in the apartment when the outdoor flood lights flash on. They're on a motion sensor and turn on now and then, but I'm surprised to see them triggered so late.

Feeling an obligation to at least get my ass up and check, I peek out the corner of the curtain to see what's going on. I'm not surprised to see Tyler jogging across the long driveway to get to his car. Looks like he's on the prowl.

I hope he finds what he's looking for.

The ringing of my phone pulls me out of a sexy dream. It's one of the first sexy dreams I've had in a month, so I'm more than a little pissed when I paw around on my nightstand to find my phone.

Dad's face flashes across my screen, and I have to pick up. It's been a few weeks since I've talked to him, and I used to call every four or five days. "Hey, Dad."

"Hi, son. Am I catching you at a good time?"

"Yeah, it's good. I'm just waking up." He has access to my shift calendar and knows when I'm off-duty, but with all the overtime I've been taking, he always assumes I'm at work.

"Did you move into that new place yet?"

"Yeah, spent the night here last night for the first time. It's a nice little apartment. You'll have to come see it sometime."

"Yeah, I'll do that." He won't do that. Dad doesn't leave Colorado Springs. Ever. He's almost seventy and doesn't drive on the freeway or at night anymore. In fact, I should go with him to his next eye appointment to make sure it's still safe for him to be driving at all.

"So, how are you doing?" He calls to check in but doesn't always have a lot to say. That just makes me feel guilty for not visiting more often. I know he's lonely.

"Good, good. Just wanted to make sure you were okay with your new living arrangements."

"Yeah, I'm good, Dad." I stretch and sit up in bed, looking out at the light drizzle falling. "I was thinking I'd head over to see you next week. Does that work for you?"

"You know I don't go anywhere." Dad laughs and then coughs a few times into the phone. "But if you tell me when you're coming, I'll see if Ana can bake one of her pies."

"Ana?" I smile at the cheery tone in Dad's voice. "Who's Ana?"

"You know Ana." I can picture him waving me off as if I'm being ignorant. "She lives across the street and two houses over."

"Mrs. Martinez?" I didn't realize they were friends. At least not the kind of friends that can request homemade pies.

"Yeah, Ana Martinez."

"Um, does Mr. Martinez know she's baking pies for you?" I try not to laugh out loud at the idea of my dad getting involved in some geriatric love triangle.

"Probably not since he's been dead for two years."

"Oh, shit. Sorry."

"He was old. It happens." Dad has always had a fatalistic attitude. Not in an unhealthy way, but he accepts that he's at the final phase of his life. He's okay with moving on when his time comes.

The concept is a little harder for me to accept. I had to witness Dad's "Do Not Resuscitate" order as part of his living will, and I'm still not comfortable with it. I wouldn't ever expect him to live on life support if he wasn't going to have a meaningful quality of life, but it scares the hell out of me to think that he could have a minor fall and the paramedics would be limited in their ability to help him.

At twenty-nine, I'm too young to be thinking about becoming an orphan. But that's what will happen when Dad's gone. He doesn't have any family, and Mom's family has all written me off.

Mom was raised in a very religious Southern family. When she found out I was gay, she wanted to put me out on the street. Dad didn't let her, so she left us both.

If he's ever resented me for having to choose me over his wife, he's never shown it. Despite being almost twenty years older than my mom, he's very open minded. He just wants me to be happy and healthy. I just wish he didn't have to give up his own happiness to ensure mine.

"Okay, well, I'll let you know for sure what day, but it'll probably be Saturday or Sunday."

"Any day is fine. I'll just be watching movies. You can come anytime."

"Alright, Dad. I should probably get up and start unpacking."

"Make sure you disinfect the cabinets before you use them. Don't know what the past tenants kept in them."

I hold in a chuckle. What the hell is he talking about? Sometimes his age does show, and I worry about his mind. "Okay, Dad. Will do. Love you."

"Love you too, son. Be safe."

CHAPTER SIXTEEN

TYLER

I don't know why I thought I'd see more of Josh once he was living upstairs. During his first three nights at home, I hardly saw him at all. And now he's back at work for four days. Even though it seems like I'm stalking him, I'm really not. He gave me access to his cloud calendar so I know when he's around. He said it was so we could keep an eye on the apartment when it's empty, but the way his eyes lingered on my mouth when I was talking made me wonder if there was more to it. I'd like to think he's making it easy for me to see him.

Yes, I know I'm reaching. But reaching is what I do. I'm a fiction writer. I make up stories. Usually, they're on paper. Sadly, this time, it's a running fantasy in my mind. A fantasy in which I'm out of milk and run over to Josh's place to borrow a cup. Obviously, he's just getting out of the shower and wearing nothing but a towel around his waist. I offer to wait on the landing, but Josh is too polite to make me wait outside. He invites me in while he pours some milk into a travel mug. While he's screwing the lid on the mug, his towel loosens and falls to his feet, revealing his thick erection.

Since his hands are full, I bend down to pick up the towel and reattach it. But once I'm on my knees, I forget about the towel and attach my lips to his fat dick instead. Of course, the fantasy usually fades with us fucking against the counter and on the floor before we move to his bed.

I haven't managed to last longer than the point of Josh coming deep inside me, breeding me in an act of possession. But I know how I want the fantasy to end. The same way I want my reality to end.

With Josh opening his heart to me as more than just a friend.

But, some fantasies aren't meant to come true. I just hope this one isn't that kind.

The alarm bell chimes, so I look at the front door to greet my customer. I'm surprised to see Britney and Harper coming in. Britney looks a little thinner than the last time I saw her, but Harper seems clean and healthy. Mom will be relieved. I send her a quick text.

Britney and Harper are here.

Mom's visiting with some customers upstairs, but she's been anxious to check on these girls.

Be right down. Don't let them leave.

"Hey, Britney. It's good to see you."

"Oh, thanks." She seems surprised that I remember her name. She might also be a little uncomfortable by it, but she doesn't look as panicked as she did the first few times she came in. "You too."

"How are you guys doing?" I don't really know how to make small talk with teen moms, but I can hear my own mom jogging down the stairs so I know I'll be rescued soon.

"We're good. I'm engaged now." She holds out her left hand and shows me the silver band on her ring finger. "As soon as my fiancé gets back from training, we're getting married, and we can finally get an apartment."

"That's wonderful!" Mom gushes as she throws her arms around Britney, almost knocking the unsuspecting girl to the ground. "I'm so happy for you."

"Thanks." Britney looks at me with an unsure grin. She clearly isn't used to maternal affection. That makes me sad.

"Well, you came at the right time. Tyler was just about to go get donuts for everyone. He'll be right back. Won't you, dear?"

"Absolutely. I was just getting ready to leave." Apparently, it's donut day at Owl Eyes Bookstore. What will that woman think of next?

~**~

Kim is at the front counter when I get back with donuts. "You just missed your boyfriend."

"What?" I look around to see who she's talking to. I'm on the only one around, so I look back at her. "Who?"

She points up and toward the back of the building. "The new tenant. He just left."

"Josh? He was here?" He should be at work today. "Is everything okay?"

Kim's smile grows as she stares at me. "Wow, you're crushing hard."

"What?" I can feel my cheeks pinking up. "Am not."

"Oh my god, you so are! Marg, you were right."

Mom peeks her head out from behind a cabinet. "I knew it. He always gets that school-boy flush when he likes someone."

"Seriously, Mom. You're worse than a twelve-year-old girl."

She just laughs, loving the comparison. She's always been young at heart and a sucker for a good love story.

"Anyway, why was Josh here? Is everything okay with the apartment?" I'm not much of a handyman, but if something's wrong, I'll find someone to fix anything I can't.

"They replaced the bin." Kim nods toward the Toys for Tots barrel. "We need to keep filling it up so I can get my weekly dose of sexy fireman. Three guys came in wearing those tight T-shirts. Damn, they're yummy."

I stand and stare at the empty barrel, disappointed that I missed a chance to see Josh. "Yeah, they are."

Kim laughs. "Are any of them straight? Because if they are, I'll personally buy a barrel of toys just to get some digits."

I ignore her comment and take the box of donuts to Mom. "Well, what do you want to do with these?"

She sighs loudly at my incompetence. "They need to go to the children's section. Can you set up a table over there?"

"Sure thing, Mom." I'm sure Britney and Harper really need more sugar and empty calories in their diets. "Maybe the next care package should have toothpaste and toothbrushes. Dentists are expensive."

Mom gives me a dirty look, but I can tell she's feeling a little guilty. "Fine. Next time, we'll do a fruit salad."

CHAPTER SEVENTEEN

JOSH

By the time I get home from my shift, I'm exhausted. I barely drag my ass up the stairs then head straight to bed. I want to sleep all day, but I need to get to the gym before noon. Working out at the station is great, but I've been slacking off on my cardio when I'm not working. And with a fitness test coming up, I need to put in more miles than I have been.

After setting the alarm on my phone for ten thirty, I strip out of my clothes and curl up in bed for a nice nap. At least, that's the plan. After about two minutes, I realize there's a problem. A problem that's getting more and more annoying as the days go on.

I'm fucking horny!

And it's been difficult to deal with it lately. I'm not much of an exhibitionist. I've had sex outdoors exactly one time and given a front seat hand job only twice in my life. I'm very conservative when it comes to sex. I just like to keep some things private. Which is why I almost never jack off in the firehouse.

All the other guys do it. I know no one would notice or care if I did too. But I just can't bring myself to do it unless I'm really horny. And I did it four times on this last shift.

That's more than I've jacked off at home in the past month. Well, not in the most recent month, but in the month before my breakup.

I keep telling myself I'm just lonely. Toward the end, Matt and I didn't have sex as often as we used to, but we still did it at least once a week. Most of the time.

And that was good enough.

I like waiting for gratification. I like feeling that slow urge build up to a desperate ache for climax.

But for the last week, all I can think about is getting off. And instead of the usual amateur couple porn I used to watch, I've been gravitating to the more scripted stuff. Nothing crazy. Just the pizza boy peeping through a window or the locker room banter turning into a steamy fuck.

But that isn't my problem.

My problem is that no matter what video I'm watching or what's playing out in my mind, Tyler's face keeps showing up.

I know it's stupid to let myself fantasize about something I can never have. He's too close. If he was a far acquaintance that I never saw, it would be harmless to entertain these kind of thoughts. But that's not the case.

Every minute that I'm at home, I know he's just feet away from me. Either working in the same building or at his home just across the courtyard.

None of these arguments soften my cock so I give in to one last release before I can finally nap. I dig out a tube of hand lotion from my nightstand and squirt a dollop into my palm. The fantasy in my head already starts rolling before I've even touched myself.

A mop of blond hair is buried between my thighs as Tyler flicks his tongue across my balls. They immediately tighten, loving the attention from such a skilled mouth. When my fingers close around my shaft, I see Tyler's smaller hand gripping me. The lotion makes my hand feel silky smooth, just how I imagine Tyler's skin feels.

There isn't rough friction like I'm used to from Matt. No, this is soft and slow. Sensual in a way I've never felt before. My hips start to thrust back and forth, moving into the hole I've created with my hand to mimic

Tyler's mouth...or is it his ass? Either way, it's him. It's always him when I work my shaft up and down until I finally shoot onto my chest.

Fuck, now I have to change these sheets.

But it was worth it. Each climax feels better than the last. It's almost scary that they seem to be building up to something.

Something physical between Tyler and me.

And as much as my body might want to just go for it, my heart knows better. I can't do casual. I don't want to do casual.

But I do want to do Tyler.

So where the fuck does that leave me?

~**~

I skip the gym and go for a run. There are several trails and parks around the bookstore that make it an ideal location to get in five miles. On my cool down walk back home, I pass by a deli and almost stumble over my own feet. Tyler is sitting inside with his laptop, and he looks so damn cute.

I stop and stare into the window for a minute, debating whether or not to go inside. The Apple Pay sticker in the window makes the decision easy since I don't have my wallet with me.

I push open the door and step inside, wondering if I should pretend not to see Tyler yet or if I should just walk up to him and say hi. Before I decide either way, Tyler looks up and catches my eye. His smile is instant and goes all the way to his eyes. And then those eyes change from twinkling to smoldering as they roam down my sweaty body.

Fuck, I'm sweaty and gross. I shouldn't have come in here. I probably smell like a damn billy goat. Shit, shit, shit.

Tyler waves me over then lowers his laptop screen. "Hey, Josh. How's it going?"

"Good." I stand as far away as I can so he doesn't get a whiff of my sweat. "Just finished a run and decided to grab a sandwich."

"Oh, wanna join me? I hate always eating alone."

Well, I can't exactly say no to that. "Sure. Let me go order. Do you need anything else?"

Tyler holds up his full bottle of water. "Nope, I'm good."

As soon as I'm seated across from him, I notice Tyler has a notebook tucked under his laptop. "Are you studying for something?"

He looks startled by the question but recovers quickly. "No, not studying. Just a little project I'm working on."

I want to ask what it is. But if he wanted me to know, he would have explained in a less cryptic way. I just nod and take a look around the deli. "It's not too busy in here."

"Uh, yeah."

Great, he thinks I'm an idiot because I can't make small talk.

"I just mean, it's a quiet place to work." Oh, that's much better. I'm a damn philosopher over here.

Thankfully, Tyler just laughs. "So, are you all settled in upstairs? Are there any issues with the apartment?"

"Not at all. It's great." I hope I don't sound too excited, but I really am. It's a perfect bachelor pad and much cheaper than the mortgage I expected to be in by now.

"Good." Tyler rolls the edge of his water bottle on the table for a second before looking up at me. "Hey, I was wondering if you want to grab a pizza tonight. Maybe watch a movie or something."

"Yeah!" The word is out of my mouth before I can stop it. This is exactly what I shouldn't be doing. Hanging out with Tyler, especially at night...in my apartment, is going to end with me doing something I'm going to regret. Either I'll sleep with him and things will be awkward when he moves on, or I won't and I'll continue to harbor this unhealthy infatuation with him. Either scenario is bad, but that doesn't stop my mind from wanting to pursue one of those regrets...badly.

"Great." Tyler looks thoughtful for a moment while holding his lower lip between his teeth. "I usually work until nine, but since that's kinda late, I can come over at six. I just have to run down at nine for about twenty minutes to get everything locked up."

"Don't you need to be there?" Tyler mentioned that he doesn't like to make his mom work alone at night.

"No, Darren will be there. He can work alone. It's not like we'll be far. If there's an emergency, he can just scream and we'll hear him."

That's good to know. I like the idea of knowing that if Tyler ever needs me while he's in the store, he can just scream, and I'll be there. At least on the days I'm home.

CHAPTER EIGHTEEN

TYLER

The past two weeks have been amazing. Every night that Josh is home, we find some reason to hang out. We've gone to the movies a few times, started watching past seasons of Survivor, and tonight, he's coming to our house for dinner. Mom is doing fondue night, and there is always too much food for just the two of us. She even invited Chad to come.

I'm glad Chad accepted the invitation, but now I'm not sure if Mom is trying to set me up with one of those two firemen or if she's trying to set them up with each other. That thought doesn't sit well so I open up my manuscript and make the last batch of edits from my editor. I only have a few more days before I need to upload book eight in the Glass Bay series, but it's in good shape. I finished it about a week earlier than usual. I think that's because of my new inspiration. In this book, Jaxon is investigating a string of arsons in Glass Bay and spends a lot of time with a handsome firefighter named Sean.

I'm worried that Chad or Josh might recognize similarities between Sean and Josh. But that's crazy. Everyone can find some similarities between themselves and fictional characters if they look close enough. And honestly, part of me almost hopes they do.

Although I don't think I'll ever come out and tell anyone I'm Rex Calloway, a small piece of me hopes someone will figure it out. That a careless mistake will out me so I can just tell everyone the truth and move on without the deception.

Of course, I'm also worried that Jaxon coming out as gay, or clearly being attracted to Sean, might ruin the series for some readers. I've tried to attract an open-minded fan base, but who knows what will happen when the women who have fallen for Jaxon realize he plays for the other team.

Well, it might make or break the series, but it's time. Jaxon's gonna have a crush.

And speaking of crushes, here come Josh and Chad now. A small spark of jealousy burns in my belly when Josh opens the door for Chad to enter, but I don't dwell on it. Josh isn't mine and probably never will be.

"Hey, guys." I glance at the time on my laptop. "Good timing. Mom should be ready for us in a few minutes. You can head over if you want. I just need to close up what I'm doing here."

"No worries, man." Chad fist bumps me from across the counter. "We can hang out here for a minute."

"How's it going today?" Josh asks, looking around the store.

"It's been busy all day but things are quiet right now. The calm before the storm." My tone gets low and ominous, making Josh smile. I love making him smile. "The calm before the storm."

"Yeah, thanks for that," Darren calls out from the reference section. "I don't need any storm coming tonight. I want a chill night."

Before I can respond, the door opens, and a cry fills the room. All heads turn to see Britney struggling to push a large baby stroller through the door while Harper fidgets in her arm. Her casted arm.

Josh immediately grabs the door while Chad helps pull the stroller inside. It's loaded down with blankets and backpacks. It looks like they're in the middle of moving.

"Hey, Britney." I step closer to offer some assistance but I'm not sure how to help. Mom is much better at this stuff than I am. "Everything okay?"

"Yeah." She tries to cover up her flustered entrance by placing Harper on her feet. "We just wanted to see if you have any new books."

"Yeah, of course." I watch Harper run toward the children's section. She's been here often enough to know exactly where to go. "What happened to your arm?"

She instinctively slides her arm behind her back, as if we might forget about the cast if we can't see it anymore. "Um, I had a little accident. Nothing serious. Just a small fracture."

Chad shifts his weight then takes a few steps back, peeking around the corner to check on Harper. I can tell he wants to say something but he keeps his mouth shut.

Britney pulls her heavy coat off and slips it over the back of the stroller, piling it on top of everything else she has in there. I can hold in a small gasp of air when I see her baby bump. It's not huge but on her small, undernourished frame, there's no mistaking it for bloat. "Sorry... Um, congratulations." I don't know what else to say. This seems like a worst case scenario for a girl in her situation.

"Thanks." Her palm immediately cups her lower belly. "Yeah, we weren't expecting to have another baby so soon."

Chad finally speaks up. "Your husband must be excited."

Britney forces a smile that looks suspiciously pained. That's when I notice the faint bruising on her cheeks. "Well, like I said, we weren't expecting it. Things have been tough with Harper. But we're getting married soon, and things will be a lot easier after that. We'll have insurance and everything."

"Have you been to a doctor yet?" Chad is a dichotomy. One second he seems furiously pissed, and the next, he seems gentle and caring.

She shakes her head. "All they'll tell me at this point is that I'm pregnant." She laughs and points to her protruding belly. "And I already know that. I remember everything from the first time around. As long as we have insurance by the time my water breaks, I think we'll be fine."

I'm speechless. I wish Mom was here. She'd know how to convince this girl to get proper medical care. Hell, she probably has a bottle of vitamins she could offer to replace some of the nutrients Britney isn't getting from her daily diet.

But Mom's not here, and we're a bunch of gay dudes who don't seem to have a clue what to say.

"Um, I better go check on Harper." Britney pushes the loaded-down stroller around the corner and disappears.

Both Chad and Josh look at me with accusing eyes, like I'm harboring a teen runaway. Instead of saying anything to them while we're just a few feet away from her, I motion for them to follow me out the back door.

"Darren, I'm out. I'll see you at nine."

CHAPTER NINETEEN

JOSH

What the fuck was that all about? Chad is stomping through the yard like he's personally offended, and Tyler looks shell shocked.

It's not clear what his relationship with those two young women is, but I hope he plans on explaining it right the fuck now.

"Mom, we're here," Ty calls into the house while holding the door open for me and Chad. "And you're not gonna believe what I have to tell you."

"In here." We follow Ty into the dining room. Marge already has the large table full of food when we walk

171

in. "What took you so long? I was just about to march over there to get you."

"Britney came in." Tyler drops the words like a bomb. "And she's pregnant."

Marge gasps and covers her mouth. Her reaction is oddly similar to Ty's, which makes me even more curious about their relationship. "Oh, no."

"And she has a broken arm." Tyler is acting like an older brother tattling on a sibling. It might be cute if the situation didn't seem so tragic.

"Dammit!" Marge pounds her fist on the table and narrows her eyes. "I knew it. I knew there was something going on with that boyfriend of hers."

"You think her boyfriend hurt her?" Chad's fists clench before he folds his arms across his chest and tucks them under his pits. "She said they're getting married."

Marge just shakes her head and slinks into the chair she's standing beside. "I don't know for sure, but I think she's homeless. Maybe staying at the shelter but she won't tell us much."

Tyler goes to his mom's side. "She hasn't seen a doctor about the baby. She said she's waiting until they get medical insurance."

"My god. What is she thinking?" Marge turns on the fondue pot to start melting the cheese. "You boys get started on dinner. I'm going to go check on her and see if she needs anything. Maybe I can talk her into coming back to eat with us."

We all watch in silence while Marge packs up a container of boiled potatoes, baby carrots and French bread before disappearing out of the room.

Chad and I both turn to Tyler. He looks sick as he tells us about how Britney and Harper first came into the store looking hungry and dirty. Apparently, they continue to come back now and then to hang out and get a meal.

"So, she might be living on the streets?" Chad asks the question on the tip of my tongue.

Tyler shrugs. "I don't think so. She's never that dirty, and the baby seems to be eating okay. I just don't think they're in a good situation."

"How old is she? She looks young." If I had to guess, I'd say the girl was only sixteen or seventeen.

"She said she graduated high school last summer. That's when she moved away from her parents." Tyler took a bite of bread dipped in melted cheese. "We're assuming she's eighteen but we don't know for sure."

"What can we do?" Chad looks broken. I've never seen him so upset. He's always the one who jokes through awkward or uncomfortable situations.

"I wish I knew." We all turn to see Marge walking in with a defeated look on her face. "She's so stubborn. She truly believes this idiot is going to take care of her and two babies."

Chad stands up, sliding his chair back loudly from the table. "Are they still here?"

Marge nods her head. "They're going to read a few more books. She's trying to get Harper to fall asleep before they leave."

Chad nods. "I'll be right back."

I stand and reach for his arm, holding him back for a minute. "You sure? You want me to go with you?"

He shakes his head. "I just want to make sure she's aware of her options. I'll be okay."

We're all quiet for several minutes after Chad disappears. Then Marge breaks the silence. "So, how's the cheese?"

Tyler looks at me, and we both bust up laughing. I'm not sure either of us know why, but the tense moment has finally passed.

"So what are you boys doing for Halloween?"

"When is Halloween?" I try to remember what day it is. The past few days have been a blur.

"This Friday. I'm going to visit my sister in Salt Lake so you guys will have to keep an eye on the place." Marge dishes the last of the broccoli onto my plate after loading up Tyler's.

My jaw is slack as I look at my plateful of veggies. When I look at Tyler, he's smiling back at me. "Mom doesn't like to waste healthy food."

The corner of my mouth pulls up, and a small lump forms in my throat. "Thanks, and yeah, we'll keep an eye on things here." I haven't had a mom taking care of me in a long time. It feels good.

Tyler saves me from the spotlight by moving the conversation back to his mom's question. "I might go out. I don't know for sure yet."

Of course he will. I clear my throat and dip a broccoli spear into the cheese. "I'll probably be working. I usually am."

"You're not scheduled for that night." Tyler blurts out the words then flinches back when he realizes what he's just said. "I mean, it's a week from today so you should be off, right?"

I hold his gaze, enjoying the feeling in my gut that's only there when Tyler does something sweet. Or flirty. Or awkward, like right now.

CHAPTER TWENTY

TYLER

The reviews are mixed. Most people knew that Jaxon was gay from the beginning, but there are still a few readers that can't quite accept it. I'm sure I've lost a few, but the sales have actually doubled with this release. It was a slow news month, and the New York Times did a full article on the official coming out of one of America's most eligible fictional bachelors.

"Did you know?" Josh startles me as I'm shelving the paperbacks of the new book.

"Know what?" I feign ignorance as he pulls a copy from the box I'm unpacking and flips to the back cover.

"That Jaxon's gay?"

"I had the same suspicions everyone else did." I lean back, resting my weight on my heels. "Were you surprised?"

Josh's eyes lock on mine, and he doesn't break eye contact as he slowly shakes his head. "Not at all."

Okay. Why do I feel like he's saying more?

"Have you read the book already?" I know I haven't sold him a copy. In fact, I have one stashed under the counter for him.

"I got anxious and read it on my phone." He cocks an eyebrow. "I might even invest in one of those tablet reader things. No one gives you shit about what you're reading when they can't see the covers."

I nod in agreement. "My ereader is one of my favorite toys."

Josh's smile grows wider, and a slight flush creeps up his cheeks. "Do you have a lot of toys?"

Holy shit. Is Josh Douglas actually flirting with me? "A bag full."

"A whole bag?" He chuckles under his breath. I'm tempted to take a whiff to see if he's been drinking. Josh has *never* acted this way before. I love it.

Josh shakes his head, and his smile fades just for a second before he forces it back. "Yeah, I shouldn't be surprised by that."

"What do you mean?" I think I should be offended, but I'm not sure why.

"Nothing." Josh pulls back the front cover and runs his fingers over the title page. "I'll let you get back to work. I just wanted the hard copy for my collection."

His collection? Josh has a collection of my books.

If only he'd add *me* to it...

~**~

No matter how hard I try, I can't convince Josh to go to the Unicorn with us for their Halloween bash. He doesn't have to work, but he claims he'll hang out at the station to hand out candy if they get a call. "We can't disappoint the kids."

I'm frustrated that I won't see him tonight, but I don't even bother trying to change his mind. How can I argue against trick or treating kids? "If you finish up early, you know where to find us."

Josh mumbles something on his way out the door. Yeah, I'm not going to see him again until morning. But that's probably for the best. I need a hookup, and since he isn't interested, I'll have to rely on one of my regulars. But the thought of doing that in front of Josh just seems wrong.

I don't know how much respect he has for me now, but I know it'll be even lower if he catches me climbing out of the back of yet another Town Car.

~**~

As soon as I have a drink in my hand, and two sips of it in my belly, I squeeze through the crowd to find my friends. Most of the people I consider to be social friends were met at this bar. Either they're past or present bartenders or they're past and present fucks.

Unfortunately, most of the guys I like most are already spoken for. Some are in long-term relationships and others brought dates for the night. Finn and Marco invite me to join in on their fun, but I'm not in the mood for that tonight.

To be honest, I'm not in the mood for anything. I just want to go home. But that's not an option. I need to get laid tonight, and I'm not going home before that happens.

"Excuse me, Officer." A deep voice invades my left ear, causing me to startle. "I'd like to confess to a crime."

The stranger's hip brushes over my barely covered dick. I knew when I put on this Naughty Cop costume that I'd get a lot of attention. But now that it's happening, it's mostly annoying.

Here to get laid.

Here to get laid.

Here to get laid.

I've got to keep my eye on the prize. I need to focus on my goal.

"Oh yeah?" I slip the handcuffs out of my booty shorts. "What crime is that?"

"Indecent thoughts about a member of law enforcement."

Dear god, this guy should be arrested for his pathetic pickup lines. But at least he's making it easy for me. I can get what I need and be back in bed before midnight. "You'll need to be a little more specific, sir."

His wide palm flattens across my bare back as he presses me against his chest. "Maybe I can buy you a drink, and we can talk about it some more."

I hold up my full glass then throw it back, eager to get this party started. "Good timing. I just finished mine."

"What's your name, baby?"

It's a little early in the night for him to be calling me baby, but he's a means to my end. And I need to get his means in my end ASAP so I can get out of this ridiculous getup and go to sleep. "Tyler."

"Well, Tyler, you can call me Daddy." Great. Just what I need. Some bossy top with control issues.

"Okay, Daddy."

"Let's go get those drinks."

~**~

I'm drunk. I don't usually let myself get drunk, but knowing that my goal was to get fucked by this

185

stranger made me a little looser when it came to accepting drinks.

"Do you live nearby?" Daddy asks me.

"I do." I lick up the shell of his ear as we slow dance to my favorite George Michael song.

"Let's go there."

Alarm bells go off, and I know I need to focus so I don't do something stupid. "Don't you have a car?" I nibble on his earlobe, hoping to make him more eager to get this over with.

I hear a soft chuckle before I feel his hot breath on my neck. "Yeah, a tiny little 'Vette. Trust me, it won't be comfortable for either of us."

I pull back and look him right in the eye. What should I do? I have the house to myself all weekend. Of course, that doesn't make this a good idea.

But, no one ever accused me of being full of good ideas. "Yeah, okay. We can do that."

Despite my better judgment, which isn't so good in my alcohol-induced haze, I let him lead me out the front door.

Chad is walking in as I walk out. He takes a look at the man I'm with and raises an eyebrow, silently questioning me. It's one thing for me to be stupid with club regulars. But this guy is a stranger. This is extra stupid.

Turning to Chad, I smile and wink. "See ya around."

~**~

As soon as we get in his car, I start to sober up. It's a blessing and a curse because the second he puts my address in his GPS, the reality of what I'm doing hits me.

Hard.

This isn't just me taking some guy back to a college dorm or low-rent apartment. I'm taking him to my mother's house...and our business.

Fuck! What am I thinking?

"You know, maybe this isn't a good idea." I sit straighter in the passenger seat and try not to let my nerves betray me. "Maybe we should head back to the club?"

He doesn't even look away from the traffic. "We'll just have a cup of coffee and talk."

Well, shit. Now what do I do? He already has my address. It's not like I can direct him to a different house and try to ditch him once the car stops.

"Um, actually, I just remembered that my roommates will be home. They hate when I bring people over. Let's grab a hotel room. We'll have more privacy."

He finally looks at me with an expression somewhere between annoyed and amused. "You said you had the house to yourself this weekend."

"I did?" Did I say that out loud? "Well, I forgot that one roommate is home. A firefighter. He's really big and mean if I wake him up. Come on. There's a Hyatt just up this street. It's my treat."

Again, he doesn't even look at me. We're getting closer, and I need to think fast. "What's your name, anyway?"

The glare he shoots me this time is definitely annoyed, no doubt about it. "I told you to call me Daddy. That's all you need to know, boy."

I consider reaching for my phone to call Josh but it's tucked in my left back pocket. There's no way I can grab it without drawing his attention.

Fuck, fuck, fuck!

CHAPTER TWENTY-ONE

JOSH

I can hear the rumble of a big-block engine several seconds before headlights illuminate the small courtyard separating the bookstore from the main house. Tyler's car is parked in the driveway, and Marge isn't going to be home until Sunday night, so I turn off the lights in my apartment and crack a window.

Eavesdropping is a character flaw that I'm not ashamed to succumb to now and then. Okay, maybe I am ashamed of it but that doesn't stop me from watching intently as a late-model 'Vette pulls up in front of the house.

Damn. Ty definitely isn't slumming it tonight.

Yeah right. A guy like him never slums it. He can walk into a room and have his pick of any man or woman he's in the mood for. And it looks like he's in the mood to party tonight.

The car barely rolls to a stop before Tyler throws open the passenger door and glances up at my apartment. Sitting in the dark, I'm pretty sure he can't see me. But something about the look on his face makes me wonder if he's in trouble.

Although, I don't spend too much time looking at his face. Once he's standing, I get a full view of the costume he's wearing...or rather what he's not wearing. The only parts of his body that are covered are his perky ass in a pair of underwear-like shorts and his shoulders in some kind of cut-off polo shirt.

Holy fuck, he's gorgeous.

I slide the window up a little farther so I can hear what they're saying. Tyler turns to the guy and places his palms on his chest to stop him from proceeding forward. "Look, I'm sorry to be a tease, but I don't think this is gonna happen."

"Don't be silly." The man closes one hand around Tyler's wrist and pulls it to his side. "This is going to happen. It'll be fun."

Tyler looks up at my apartment one more time, and even in the dim moonlight, I can see he's scared. I grab the first pair of shorts I find at the top of my hamper and step into them. They aren't even fully over my ass before I fling open my door and call down to the courtyard.

"Hey, Tyler. I need to talk to you about something."

Both men look over at me, equally shocked but for different reasons. The man releases Tyler from his grip and takes a step back. Tyler also steps away but in my direction. "Yeah. I can come up. My friend was just dropping me off."

I can almost feel the rage boiling out of this strange man as he strides back to his car. His car door slams hard once he climbs back inside.

"Thanks." Tyler flinches when the engine fires up. "Can I go up to your place for a minute?"

I nod to Tyler but don't say a word. I'm too pissed. My arms are crossed over my bare chest as I stare down the man, watching him tear out of the driveway.

Once the sound of the engine completely fades, I turn back to Tyler. "Nice friend you have there."

He rolls his eyes and turns to the staircase leading up to my apartment. "I know. It was stupid for me to bring him back here."

"So why did you?" I'm still mad but my tone softens enough to make me worried it sounds...vulnerable. And that's definitely not how I want to sound right now. "He didn't seem like the gentle type."

Tyler barks out a laugh and walks straight to my couch, falling heavily onto one side of it. "Why do you think?"

And now I'm pissed again. Am I PMSing or what? "Because your usual fuck pad was otherwise occupied?"

Tyler gasps as if I've just slapped him. I guess I did in a way, and I regret it immediately. "Sorry. That was uncalled for."

Despite the hurt in his eyes, he just laughs. "Because I'm fucking horny, okay?" He waves a hand in front of his chest. "A guy has needs, ya know. Just because you don't need to get laid, doesn't mean the rest of us have such self-control."

"Seriously?" I drop onto the far side of the couch. "You're willing to risk your life just to get off?"

Tyler's eyes flit to my chest then drop down, lingering in my lap. "Well, it's not like you're interested in helping a brother out."

Is he joking? "I just came out of a long relationship...we were about to be fucking married. I can't just have sex with the first hot guy that I meet."

Tyler's grin is back, all signs of his earlier frustration gone. "You think I'm hot?"

Shit. He's going to be the death of me. "Of course you're hot, Ty. That's why every guy wants you." I turn away, unable to look at him. "I saw how every man was watching you that night at the Unicorn."

"How?" He's teasing me now. Bastard.

"How, what?"

"How do you know other guys were looking at me?"

I fling my head back on the couch and close my eyes. "Because I was fucking watching you too. The whole goddamn night."

Without opening my eyes, I feel the cushions dip and I know Tyler is moving closer. "Then maybe you can help me out."

I shake my head. "I can't just sleep with you."

"The hell you can't." Tyler straddles my lap, forcing me to open my eyes. I have to scoot back to make sure my growing erection doesn't touch him...or his. "We're both consenting adults. And we want each other. It doesn't have to mean anything."

"It doesn't..." Of course it has to mean something. Sex means something. Doesn't it? Doesn't it mean love...or at least lust? Well, I definitely have the lust part down.

Without letting my brain stop me, I reach for Tyler's hips and slide him closer, flush with my body. His hard cock lines up perfectly with mine as I crush my lips over his.

Fuck, this is what I need.

Within seconds, we're panting and rutting against each other like dogs in heat. I wrap my hands around Tyler's head, pulling him closer into our kiss. The heat between us is primal as he grinds into my lap, causing my cock to swell, desperate for release.

"Damn," Tyler says when he pulls back from my lips. His eyes search mine, and the lust boiling behind his gaze causes an instinctive, guttural moan to rise from my throat. My hands drop down to his shoulders and tug the cut-off shirt he's wearing above his head.

I bring my lips to his firm chest, licking around his nipples as his hand rakes through my hair and down the back of my neck. When his nails reach my back, I shudder as chills run up and down my body. By the time my lips find his again, Tyler's hard cock is pressing against my dick, and he grinds us together.

"Fuck, Ty…" I'm unable to utter another word as he slips off my lap and moves down to the floor. Once again, my skin tingles as his fingers trail down my chest and land right above the shorts I put on earlier. My breath hitches when his fingertips dip below the fabric, allowing my dick to spring free.

Tyler doesn't skip a beat. He manages to pull my shorts down in a swift motion and sheath my throbbing cock with his hand. He leans between my spread legs, using his tongue to trace up my inner thigh to my balls. He licks each one lightly before dragging a trail of wet heat up my shaft all the way to the crown. His tongue is warm and smooth as it flicks around my slit, teasing my head and causing my cock to twitch under his touch.

When my shaft disappears down his throat, my head hits the back of the couch. I moan as Tyler's mouth works up and down my length, slicking me with his saliva. Grabbing a handful of his blond hair, I force him down deeper. Fucking his mouth hard and fast.

Tyler surprises me and takes all seven thick inches of my cock without even a slight gag reflex. Worried that he might not be able to breathe, I pull his head up to check on him. Like a fucking angel, he just looks at me and smiles.

"Do you have condoms and lube?" he asks briefly pulling off before going down for another taste.

"Side drawer." I point toward the bedroom. Tyler stands, his own thick shaft now completely free from his little shorts. The ridiculously hot shorts slide to the ground, revealing his tight bubble butt as he walks toward my room.

Am I seriously about to fuck that hot piece of ass.

Once he's back with the lube and condoms, Tyler grips my shaft again, stroking me as his lips crush into mine. My lust hasn't slackened in the least, and I'm still desperate to fuck him. In the back of my mind, I know this is a bad idea, but the head I'm thinking with now doesn't give a fuck. Bad idea or not, we're about to be balls deep inside Tyler's beautiful ass.

Tyler squeezes a large amount of lube on his hand then reaches between his legs. His eyes roll upward slightly when he fingers himself, opening up for me. What a fucking turn-on. My cock is throbbing even harder from just thinking about pounding this gorgeous man in front of me.

I grab a foil packet from the cushion and slide a condom over my dick. Tyler wraps his fingers around my sheathed cock and drizzles lube over us until his hand is freely gliding up and down me.

His mouth greets mine again as he straddles my thighs and lines my cock up with his tight opening. The tip of my cock finds his center, and I gently push up as he moves down.

"Fuck!" he cries out, causing me to stop my movements.

"Shit, I'm sorry." I don't want this to hurt but going slow is hard as fuck. "You slide down. I'll stay still."

"Dammit, you're so fucking thick."

Maybe this is karma telling me to stop things before they get out of hand. "We can—"

"No," Tyler says, staring at me. He moves his hands down to my chest, kneading my muscles as he lowers himself even farther on my shaft. After a few moments, he becomes acclimated to my girth and finds his rhythm.

I fucking hope it feels good to him because I'm loving each movement he makes.

Tyler's groans become louder as he rides my cock, taking control of the entire process. I lean back against the couch while rubbing circles on his hips with my thumbs.

He glides up and down, moving his pelvis in a figure eight motion, caressing my dick with his hole.

A drip of his precome hits my stomach, and I'm ready to blow. I grasp his weeping cock and tug at it, hoping to give him at least a fraction of the pleasure he's giving me. Without warning, Tyler throws back his head, moaning from the intensity of our fucking.

"God, that feels good. Don't stop." Tyler continues to pant as I work him to release. "Dammit." The speed of his up and down thrusts increase with each groan. The pit of my stomach begins to tighten as my shaft tingles in anticipation of the orgasm I'm trying to stave off. Each thrust from Tyler has me one step closer to busting a nut.

"Ty... I'm..."

"Yeah?"

"Yes," I reply, breathing heavily.

"Me too. Let it go, Josh."

Trying to hold for just a few more seconds, I spit in my hand then grab him again, using the extra fluid to glide up and down his shaft faster. "Come for me, Ty."

"Fuck!" Tyler's scream hits my ear about two seconds before his come coats my chest. Another stream erupts and lands across my lips and chin.

I can't help but to jut my tongue out and taste his salty spunk. His flavor pushes me over the edge of my own orgasm, and I shoot load after load into his ass. Tyler never stops riding my cock, even after he's spent his own release. His body continues to rock over me as waves of pleasure lull me into an almost comatose state.

I could stay right here forever.

Chapter Twenty-Two

Tyler

It feels like I'm backed up against an oven when I finally wake up. The room is familiar but not. And that's when I remember where I am and who's curled around my back like a heating pad.

I lift the heavy arm pinning me to the mattress up a few inches and roll underneath it, so I'm facing the beautiful wall of muscle that fucked me so good last night. Maybe he's ready for an encore.

Josh is still breathing heavily, so I know he's not awake yet. And I can only think of a few humane ways to wake up someone on a Saturday morning. Since it's too damn hot in this bed to climb beneath the covers, I settle for reaching between his legs for the fat hard-on that's pressing into my belly.

It only takes a few seconds for me to rouse the beast...and Josh wakes up too. His whole body goes still, and his eyes flash open. It seems to take a few seconds for realization to set in. And when it does, his hips respond in kind.

"Um, good morning?" His question is adorable. I can't think of any way for this to be any better of a morning so I lean in for a kiss.

"It certainly is." Josh's eyes close, and he thrusts harder, fucking my fist like it's personally offended him. "Let me make it even better for you."

Josh's fingers dig into my hip as he finally looks me in the eye. Without breaking our gaze, he comes between my fingers, coating my hand and thighs with his creamy spunk.

"God, you're even sexier when you come."

Josh flinches, apparently unsure how to take my compliment, before throwing his head back and laughing. "You are something else, Ty."

"Well, that's what I'm told." I wipe my hand off on the sheets and try to curl back into Josh's wide chest, but he holds me back.

"We shouldn't have done this."

"What? Why?" I'm trying to control my emotions, but that's not easy to hear while someone's sperm is still swimming around on your legs.

Josh rolls away from me, scooting to the far side of the bed before sitting up against the headboard. "I think you're a great guy, and you're hot as hell."

"But?" I can see where this is going, but I'm not making it easy on the man. If he's going to be an ass, he better be prepared to take my dick up it.

"I'm just... I know what you're looking for, and that's not me. I don't do casual fucks. This could never work."

"You know what, Josh?" I stand up and search for my shorts. "Fuck you!"

"Fuck me?" Josh looks genuinely surprised, like he has no idea what I'm talking about. Typical asshole.

"Yes!" I slip on the shorts that were on the floor near the door and look for my shoes. I just need to get the fuck out of here. "Fuck you!"

Josh is out of bed and hovering over me in all his naked gloriousness before I've slipped into my shoes. "I don't know what you're so pissed off about. Just because I'm not the kind of guy you're looking for, that doesn't mean we can't still be friends."

"Are you fucking kidding me?" I stare at him, wondering how I could have misjudged him so badly. He is seriously trying to call me a whore and then saying he still wants to be friends. "I've gotta go."

"No." Josh blocks the door with his wide body, his folded hands begging me to stay. Well, shit. It's not like I can physically move him.

"What?"

"Just tell me what I did wrong. Please."

Why are some men so stupid? I feel like most women would understand the problem. Hell, my mom would have smacked him silly five minutes ago.

I narrow my eyes a split second before the first tear falls. "You look at me like I'm some little fuckboy that can't keep it in his pants, but then you're the first one to flirt with me when we're alone. Why do you do that?"

He's speechless. His jaw unhinged but not moving for several long moments. He finally whispers out words that are barely audible. "I've never treated you badly, have I?"

My anger quickly dissipates, and now I just feel like shit. Maybe he really is just clueless. "Never mind, Josh. It's fine. We'll be friends and pretend this never happened."

"Really?" His eyes are hopeful, but his face is still skeptical. "So, we're okay?"

"Yeah, whatever." I brush past his body, carefully avoiding contact because I know I won't be strong enough to not molest him. "We're good."

"But what was all that—"

I hold up a hand to stop him. "Nothing. I was overreacting. We're fine. I'll see you later."

Before he can put two and two together, I bolt out of his door and straight to my house. If I'm lucky, I'll die of humiliation before I ever have to face him again.

CHAPTER TWENTY-THREE

JOSH

I screwed up. I don't know what I was thinking when I let what happened happen. All I know is that it shouldn't have, and now we're probably never gonna be the same. I've tried to make small talk with Tyler a few times in passing. Once when he was coming home from work, and twice I've made up an excuse to go to the bookstore. But he's still upset and won't say more than a few words to me.

Hopefully, after my next shift, enough time will have passed that he'll be willing to explain to me why he's still upset. Maybe then we can move past this. For now, I allow the firehouse to distract me from my life. We get an early call just after my shift begins that takes several hours. It's nothing serious, just a small kitchen fire, but I'm grateful it kills half the day. It isn't until the afternoon that Chad comes to bug me. I'm hitting the weights a little more aggressively than usual when Chad recognizes something's up.

"So, what crawled up your ass and died?" He straddles the bench next to mine.

"Nothing. Just working out." Of course, just having him nearby and willing to listen makes some of the walls I've built around my emotions start to weaken. When I start to struggle with the heavy weights, Chad steps behind my bench and easily lifts the bar up and onto the rack.

"You're not usually this stupid, so I know something's going on. How about you tell me what it is before you drop a bar across your neck and end it all?" He smirks and pretends to go soft. "Is that it, Josh? Are you suicidal? Is that what it's come down to? You're trying to end it all?"

"Shut the fuck up." I smack his knee as I swing my leg over the bench and sit up.

His playful expression changes, hardening into a mask I've only seen a few times before. "Did something happen to Tyler the other night?"

"What? What do you mean?" Chad doesn't look away. He's watching me for a reaction. "I saw him leave the club with some dude that seemed a little sketch."

I stand and take two steps away from him before turning back. "Then why the fuck did you let him leave with that guy?"

"So, something did happen?" Chad stands up and faces me, chest to chest, and my anger deflates immediately.

"No, but the guy was an asshole. I had to send him packing before they went inside the house."

"Tyler's fine?"

I nod and drop my chin to my chest. At least, he was fine before I did whatever I did to him.

I turn to get up and leave but Chad stops me. "I'm glad you were there then."

"I guess." I huff out a deep breath. "I just wish I'd left it at that." Shit. I need to learn to keep my mouth shut almost as bad as I need to keep my dick in my pants.

Chad's mouth opens, and he looks stunned. "Did you guys hook up?"

My eyes lock on Chad's. "What? Why would you ask that?"

I'm not a great liar. I know my quick answering his question with a question is a dead giveaway that something happened.

"Good for you, dude." Chad smiles wide and punches my arm. "Tyler's hot, and he's perfect for what you need. A quickie might just get you through the next few months. I'm proud of you, man."

Well, now that the cat is out of the bag, there's no sense trying to keep hiding things. I sit back down on the bench and drop my head between my shoulders. "No, it's not good. I think I ruined whatever friendship we had."

"Why?" Chad squeezes onto the bench next to me. "What'd you do?"

I blow out a long breath. "Honestly, I don't even know. He stayed the night and was ready for another round in the morning. Before we got carried away again, I stopped him."

"You did what?" Chad bangs his knee against mine. "Why?"

"I told him it was a bad idea, and then he got all pissed off and stormed out."

"Dude, what is wrong with you?"

"What are you talking about? I did the right thing. I stopped us before we made a mistake twice. He's not looking for what I have to offer, and we both know that."

"Oh god." Chad stretches his legs out in front of him then leans back, resting his weight on one hand. "You didn't say that, did you?"

"No." I try to think back to exactly what I did say. "I mean, maybe. I don't remember. What if I did? What's wrong with that?"

Chad looks disgusted by me. "Um, it sounds like you think he's a slut."

I shake my head and point my finger at Chad. "You've always told me he's a slut. I would never describe him in that way, and I don't think of him that way, but that's what you warned me about, right?"

"I wasn't trying to warn you, idiot. I was trying to encourage you to go for him. He's a good guy, and now he lives next door. He's perfect for you."

What? "How is that perfect for me? I'm looking for a relationship."

"And you know he's not?" Chad's staring me down, daring me to lie to him.

"Basically. You're the one who told me he's not."

Chad throws up his arms in frustration. "What the fuck do I know about what he wants? Maybe you should talk to him about it before you go making assumptions."

"Maybe." If he ever speaks to me again.

"You know what they say about when—"

"Don't." I hold out my hand to stop him. "I get it. If he ever talks to me again, maybe we can clear this up. But for now, I have to accept that he hates me."

CHAPTER TWENTY-FOUR

TYLER

"I was thinking of inviting Britney and Harper over for Thanksgiving. Are you okay with that?"

The question comes out of the blue, but I'm not very surprised by it. "Yeah, sure, Mom. That's fine."

"Hopefully, they have some family they'll be spending the day with, but if not, I want to make sure they get a nice meal."

I smirk and look up at her. "What about the boyfriend?"

Mom cringes and lets out a loud groan. "Yes, I suppose I'll have to invite him too."

"Maybe we'll like the guy?" I offer, knowing that the chances are pretty slim.

"Maybe." She rolls her eyes. "Oh, I don't know if Josh has family around town, but I'm pretty sure Chad doesn't, so I was thinking of inviting them as well."

"Uh-huh." I turn back to the magazine. "Whatever you want."

Mom doesn't move, and after a few seconds, she clears her throat. "Tyler, is there something you want to tell me?"

I don't look up from my magazine. "Like what?"

"You were spending every night with Josh before I went on my trip. Since I've been home, I haven't seen you guys together once. Did something happen while I was gone?"

"No, Mom. Everything is fine. We're just both busy. It's not like we can spend every minute together."

She raises an eyebrow. "You were doing a pretty good job of it last month, so what's changed?"

I swallow hard and hate that I'm having this conversation with my mother, but I don't really have anyone else to talk to about it. Flipping the pages like it's not a big deal, I open up to her. "We did hang out while you were gone, and Josh regretted it immediately. My feelings were hurt, and I'm not really sure where things stand now."

"Oh, honey." She squeezes my shoulder then rubs small circles over my back. "I think he's still vulnerable from his breakup. Maybe it's just too soon?"

Maybe, but I doubt that. "I think I just came on too strong for him, but go ahead and invite him over for Thanksgiving. I wouldn't want him sitting alone in that apartment if he doesn't have anywhere else to go."

"You're a good boy." She leans over and kisses my temple. "Thank you. And if I don't see him, will you invite him?"

I roll my eyes. "Please don't make me do that. He'll think I have an ulterior motive."

She looks into my eyes, and I know she sees my sincerity. "Okay, I'll make sure to find some time with him, but can you ask Chad?"

"Sure. He'll probably come in tomorrow when he gets off work."

"Thank you, honey."

~**~

Like clockwork, Chad shows up just after nine and heads straight to the counter. "What you got for me, man?"

"Oh." I close my laptop and walk around the counter. "Let's see... I think we have a few new releases you might like."

"Good, man." He clasps my shoulder and follows behind me as I lead him to the right aisle.

"Hey." I turn back to him. "I don't know if you have plans for Thanksgiving, but my mom wanted me to invite you over for dinner."

Whatever Chad was about to say seems lost as he stares at me. "That's so nice."

I shrug. "Well, it's usually just the two of us, so it'll be nice to have a few more faces at the table this year."

"Who else is coming?"

"We're hoping Britney and Harper can make it if they don't have other plans." I grimace as I say the next words. "And I guess we'll have to invite the boyfriend."

Chad's face hardens. "He's back in the picture?"

"What? I didn't know he was out of the picture."

Chad looks like he just said something he shouldn't have, but then he backpedals. "Well, I've talked to her a few times at the shelter, and it sounded like they broke up."

I narrow my eyes. "Is that it?" It doesn't sound like that's all he knows.

Chad looks me straight in the eye and lowers his voice. "That's all anyone needs to know."

"Bullshit. I hope you didn't throw this guy off a cliff or something." On the other hand, maybe I hope he did. "Well, then, maybe it'll just be the two of them and..."

"And what?" Chad asks, his face morphing into a smirk. "Anyone else you're inviting?"

I roll my eyes. He probably already knows about our hookup gone wrong. "Mom's inviting Josh, but I don't know if he has family he's spending the day with or not."

Chad smiles widely. "Good. That'll be good for him."

"You think he'll come?"

Chad shrugs. "He usually spends the day with his dad, but I think he'll appreciate the invitation."

I can't stop myself from whispering, "Is he okay?"

Chad puts his arm around my shoulder and leans close to my ear. "Not really. He's pretty upset that you're icing him out."

My cheeks flush in embarrassment. "So, he told you what happened?"

Chad nods. "I think you guys need to talk it out. Sounds like there might be some miscommunication going on."

I snort at his simple summation. "I don't think so. He pretty much hit the nail on the head when he said I'm too easy and not somebody he would ever get serious about."

"I knew it." Chad looks like he just won the lottery, completely excited by my admission. He pulls away and rests both hands on my shoulders. "Just talk to him. Be honest about what you want, and you guys might surprise each other."

When Thunder Rolls

CHAPTER TWENTY-FIVE

JOSH

I'm just pulling some spaghetti noodles off the stove when there's a soft knock at my door. "Coming," I call out while pouring the sauce over the noodles so they don't stick.

Without giving much thought to who it could be, I open the door and find Tyler standing on the other side.

"Hey, I'm sorry to interrupt." He's reluctant to look me in the eyes, staring down at his fidgeting fingers. "If you're busy, I can come back."

"No, not at all." I wave him in and turn back to the stove.

Tyler steps inside and closes the door behind him.

"I just made some spaghetti and meatballs." Glancing at the bag of frozen meatballs on the counter, I realize that's not exactly true. "Well, I warmed up meatballs... But if you haven't eaten, you're welcome to stay. I made plenty."

Tyler hesitates for a moment, looking between me and the pot on the stove, then nods. "Yeah, okay. I can eat."

Wow. I didn't expect him to agree. This is a good sign. Maybe we can get back to our easy friendship again. "Great, let me grab some plates, and you can help yourself to whatever you want to drink. There's probably a few beers and some Cokes in the fridge."

"Okay." Tyler opens the fridge door and peeks inside. "What do you want?"

"A beer would be good, thanks."

He pulls out two beers and waits for me to get the food plated before following me to the couch. If this were a formal dinner, I might have set up the dining table, but he and I have had many meals on my couch, so I go with that, trying to keep things casual until I know exactly what he's here for.

For a few minutes, we just dig in to our food without speaking. But after a while, Tyler wipes his mouth and turns to me. "So, the reason I stopped by is to invite you to Thanksgiving dinner."

"Really?" That's the last thing I expected him to say. In fact, I'm more than a little surprised.

Tyler seems to misread my surprise for discomfort. "You don't have to. It's not a big deal. Mom just didn't want you to be alone if you don't have other plans."

Of course. This is Marge's idea not his. But I know it took a lot for Tyler to come up here and offer this olive branch, so I'm not going to come across as ungrateful. "No, that sounds great. I really appreciate the offer, but I'll be at my dad's for lunch on Thanksgiving."

"Yeah, of course." Tyler picks up his fork and plays with his food. "That's cool."

I take a chance and reach out for him, resting my hand on his knee. "Seriously. I would love to come if I didn't have to be with my dad. He's alone most of the time."

"I understand." Tyler smiles, accepting the sincerity of my words. "Is he local? I'm sure Mom would love one more at the table. You're welcome to invite him."

"Really?" I can't believe he's suddenly being so cool. "That's great. I'll ask him. Although, he doesn't like to travel, so I doubt I can talk him into it. But I'll see what I can do."

"Cool." Tyler turns back to his plate. "Just let me know."

"Is it just you two for dinner?" Maybe they always invite their tenants to join them for holidays. It seems like a reasonable thing to do. I guess.

"Well, Chad is on-call but said he'll stop by if he doesn't have to go in to work." Tyler has a faraway look in his eyes before he turns back to me. "Hey, did you know Chad has been talking to Britney?"

Who? "Do you mean that girl with the baby we met at the store a few weeks ago?"

"Yeah." Tyler looks uncomfortable, like he has more to say but isn't sure if he should.

"What is it?" I realize my hand is still resting on his knee so I give it a gentle squeeze. "You can tell me anything."

"Oh, well, Chad just made it sound like he chased off her boyfriend or something. Do you know anything about that?"

"No way. Chad wouldn't hurt some kid." But even as I'm saying the words, my mind is pulling up an image of Chad with a bruised cheek and cuts on his right knuckles a few weeks ago. He said he took a street fighting class at his gym. At the time I believed him, but now I'm wondering what really happened.

"Yeah, you're right." Tyler relaxes his rigid body and reaches for his beer. "I guess I was probably reading more into what he didn't say than what he did. I do that sometimes, as you know."

This is it. I guess he's ready to finally talk. "About the other morning..."

"You don't have to say anything." Tyler looks mortified as he draws lines with his finger through the condensation on his can. "I completely understand how you feel. Fuck, if I were you, I'd feel the same way about a guy like me."

What the fuck is he talking about? "Um, I think you lost me." I smile to lighten some of the tension in the room. If we're going to have a difficult or awkward conversation, I'd rather do it in a slightly more relaxed manner.

"You're right. I know people think I'm an easy lay. A sure thing." He turns toward the window but not before I see the way his eyes glisten with moisture. "And they're right."

"That's not who you are, Ty." I take the plate out of his hand and set it on the table by mine. "You're a caring, gorgeous, smart man that any guy would be lucky to come home to."

He turns to look me straight in the eyes, his lower lids just barely containing the tears about to fall. "Any guy except you, right?"

"No, I'd be lucky to have you. But we're at different places in our lives. I was about to marry a cheating asshole because I crave the stability of having one man in my life. I've never been one to sleep around," I hold up my hand to shush him when he tries to interrupt me, "not because I think badly of people who do, it just never appealed to me."

"I don't get it. What does that have to do with me?" Tyler rubs the tears out of his eyes with the heels of his palms. "I mean, I know you're not a player. I get that."

"Well…" What does it have to do with him? Why am I putting all my shit on Tyler? He was just looking for a good time. He wasn't asking for a morality lecture. "I guess I just didn't want to let myself get caught up in you when you just wanted to have fun. That's totally cool and all, but I tend to equate sex with love."

"You do?" Tyler looks like he's either going to cry some more or vomit. I'm not sure which I'd prefer.

"Well, yeah. That's why I felt guilty about what we did that night. And why I didn't want to do anything else the next morning. I just knew it would make it harder for me to let you go."

Tyler rests his hand over mine. "Why would you have to let me go?" His whispered words are more vulnerable than I've ever heard him. It breaks my heart to know I'm the one forcing him to face realities neither one of us want to face.

"Because you like to go out and party. You are so much fun. You deserve to be sowing your oats until you find a man good enough to settle down with." I turn away and try to remove my hand from his grasp but Tyler just holds on tighter. "And I was already starting to fall for you."

"You are?" Tyler asks, his voice full of awe and hope. "I mean, you were?"

Looking into his clear blue eyes, I nod my head. "Are."

We just stare at each other for several long moments before Tyler leans forward and brushes his lips against mine. "Me too."

"But what about all the guys..." I close my eyes and let him kiss up my jaw, barely able to focus on the question I'm trying to ask. "The clubbing and going out. You don't want to give that up, do you?"

Tyler licks up the shell of my ear and breathes heavily into it, causing a shiver to race down my spine. "Fuck yeah, I do. I'd give it all up to be with you."

My heart is pounding, ready to beat right out of my chest. "Are you sure?"

"Definitely." Tyler bites hard on my earlobe, sending a spike of pain straight to my hardening dick. "I want you."

Chapter Twenty-Six

Tyler

A slow moan in the back of my mind is warning me to take things slow. But my dick is screaming to move as fast as possible. Even though everything got royally screwed up last time we were in this position, I can't stop. I won't. It feels too good to be back in Josh's arms.

Giving in to the need that's been causing me to ache for days, I follow Josh back to his bedroom. His eyes lock on mine as he reaches for the hem of my hoodie. I give him an almost imperceptible smile, encouraging him to go for what he wants. Without any further hesitation, Josh fully undresses me before lying me down on his bed.

"You're so beautiful." His whispered praise means more to me than when I've heard the same words from other men. They've said it to make me feel good in the moment. Josh isn't just trying to get in my pants. He says what he means—good or bad—which makes the weight of his words so much more powerful.

"So are you. Inside and out." Although, I'm anxious to see some of his outside. Now.

As if reading my mind, Josh slowly strips out of his clothes, giving me plenty of time to appreciate his thick muscles and smooth skin as it's revealed. Once he's fully naked, Josh just stands there, waiting for my eyes to eventually find their way back to his. "You ready or should I just stand here for a while longer?"

I cock my head to the side in contemplation. "I could stare at you for the rest of my life and not be ready to look away, but yes, I want you in me."

"Fuck, Ty." He spreads my knees with his leg before lower down on me. "When you talk like that, it's hard for me to be a gentleman."

I laugh out loud. "Fuck being a gentleman. I want a tough fireman who knows how to get a little rough?"

Josh moans loudly, grinding his immense cock against my thigh then scooting up so it's poking at my taint. His voice is low and husky. "You like it rough?"

"Right now I do."

He rocks into me, pressing my skin hard and causing me to squirm.

"Quit teasing, and get inside me."

Josh releases a low chuckle. "It's gonna be real rough if we don't find some lube in the next two seconds."

That sounds like two seconds too long. I roll underneath him and reach for his nightstand, pulling out the lube and condoms I know he keeps in there.

"Hurry!" I shove the lube into his hand and tear open the condom, rolling it onto his thick shaft before he even has the bottle open.

"Slow down, slugger. We have all night."

All night. I can't remember the last time someone wanted to spend an entire night holding me. Touching me. Loving me. Maybe not loving me in the heart-felt way, but with every touch across my skin and kiss along my jaw, I feel his love for what he's doing.

"If we do this, we're doing this." Josh lines up his head with my opening but his bright blue eyes are locked on mine. "I don't do casual. I do relationships. You don't have to promise me forever, but I want a promise that this is what you want. That you're going to give us a real chance."

"That's all I'm asking for." I lift up on my elbows to kiss him, slowing moving my mouth against his as he slowing breaches me. Josh doesn't bother to open me up first, and I love that. I love feeling the stretch and burn of penetration from his cock instead of his fingers.

"Is this okay?" he asks when he's just past the tight ring of muscle holding him at bay.

"It's so good. I want it all." And so he gives it to me.

He pushes deeper in small bursts, allowing me to slowly adjust to his wide girth while giving himself time to acclimate to my tight heat. "You're like a second skin I'm putting on. A perfect fit."

I smile and tilt up, bearing down on him until he's fully seated. "You definitely are."

And then he makes love to me, proving that he cares about me in way no one else has before. His gentle murmurs and passionate kisses offer more assurance of his pure intentions than any of his previous words.

And I finally allow myself to feel for someone what I've never felt before. He's been stealing slivers of my heart from the first conversation we ever had, but now it's breaking apart in large chunks and reattaching with Josh fully embedded inside.

~**~

Britney and Chad both make it to Thanksgiving dinner, making for a more lively meal than I can remember having in this house in a long time.

With just three months left before the baby is born, Britney is excited about her future. She was accepted into a work-study program at the community college that offers day care for Harper. She's still staying at the shelter because that's the only way she can stay in the program tuition-free, but she's working on an accounting certificate and hopes to be done with it by summer.

Mom has invited them to move into our guestroom, and Chad even offered to get her an apartment, but she's stubborn. I get the feeling she still has trust issues and isn't ready to accept more than a charitable meal or diapers for Harper.

But after the new baby comes, we're hopeful she realizes she needs extra help and is willing to accept it from us.

Mom and Britney bring out pies and put them on the table. Just before Mom makes the first slice, the doorbell rings. I can feel the obnoxious smile spread across my face before I'm even out of my chair.

Practically sprinting to the front door, I can't wait to see him. Josh left early this morning to head up to Colorado Springs, and I didn't get more than a quick peck before he snuck out of his bed, leaving me to sleep for another two hours in the delicious scent of his sheets.

"Hey, Happy Thanksgiving." Josh opens his arms in time for me to fall into them.

"I missed you." I barely get the words out before capturing his lips in a hard kiss. I love that we can do this now.

A loud cough behind me breaks the spell of being lost in Josh. Reluctantly, I pull away and turn to see who so rudely interrupted us. Of course, it's Chad.

His toothy grin is too cute to stay mad at. "What?"

"I'm just happy to see you guys both got your shit together."

Josh punches his arm as he passes through the doorway. "Yeah, you're next, buddy."

Chad snorts before reaching down to pick up Harper. She's been clinging to him all night. "Why would I need a boyfriend when I've got such a beautiful lady right here?" He raises her up and blows a raspberry on her belly.

Her sweet baby laugh has us all enamored. Mom has her arm around Britney, and they're having a quiet conversation on the other side of the room. They're both watching Chad fondly, and I hope Josh is right. I hope Chad is the next person to find love. He has so much of it to give.

CHAPTER TWENTY-SEVEN

JOSH - *THREE MONTHS LATER*

For the first time since I started working at the station, I hate my job. Not my job per se, but I hate leaving Ty for four days at a time. But this is one of those weird periods when he seems almost happy to see me go. I trust him in my heart, but this is the second time since we've been together that he's tied himself to his laptop and closes the screen every time I get close enough to see it.

I've never done this before, but I've never had a reason to. Well, I did have a reason to with Matt, I just didn't know it. And that betrayal keeps a slight niggle of doubt in the back of my mind. So, hoping to find out once and for all that there's nothing nefarious going on with Tyler, I sneak out of the station with my full gear in the back of my car in case we get a call. It's after eleven when I walk up the steps to the apartment I'm now sharing with Ty and quietly open the front door.

Tyler is asleep on the sofa with his laptop propped up on his lap. The screen is dark but I know just one keystroke will wake it back up. I don't want to distrust him, but I can't continue to worry. He's keeping something from me, and I need to know what it is.

With a tight knot in my stomach, I wake up the screen and try to figure out what I'm looking at. A word file takes up the whole screen, and I'm wondering if it's some kind of love letter, or worse, a "Dear John" letter.

...Jaxon turned in his resignation with a mix of excitement and nervous energy filling his heart and mind. He was about to marry Sean, devoting his life to the man he loved instead of the crimes he solved. Risking his life to help others no longer appealed. It was time to

commit himself with his whole self to Sean, forever and always.

The end.

What the hell is that? I reread the paragraph three times, still not understanding what it meant.

"So now you know." Tyler's soft whisper startles me and I step back, guilty for snooping and embarrassed for getting caught.

"Know what? What is that?"

Tyler closes the laptop and sets it on the table, sitting up to make room for me next to him. When I don't sit immediately, he pats the cushion. "Please sit with me for a minute."

I do as requested but still have no idea what he's talking about. "What's going on, Ty?"

I hate the quiver in my voice. I shouldn't feel so insecure with Tyler but I do. I love him too much to think he's breaking up with me...but the pit in my stomach has grown into a full-blown bush, thorny and tangling around my insides.

"Baby, don't look at me like that. It's not bad." Tyler closes his eyes for a few moments then braces himself to say whatever he has to say. "I'm Rex Calloway."

"What?" What does that mean? He's Tyler Kelly. I've met his mom. I know who he is. "I don't understand."

"The author, Rex Calloway. That's me. I've been writing that series for the past two years." His nervous smile helps to relieve some of my own anxiety.

"Are you serious?" That doesn't sound so bad. It actually sounds kinda cool. "You're a writer?"

Tyler shrugs bashfully and looks down at his wringing hands. "Yeah. I started writing under the pseudonym Rex Calloway, and then after they got successful, I didn't really know how to tell people it was me."

I turn back to the laptop and point to the closed screen. "So what was that? The new book?

Tyler beams with pride. "Yep. Just finished it tonight."

I replay the words I read and consider the impact of each word. "So it's over? You're done?"

"I'm done with Jaxon. He's found his happy ending. But I'm not done writing. I was thinking of doing a series about a sexy firefighter next." Tyler waggles his eyebrows, leaning against my chest and kissing my neck. "What do you think?"

"Sounds good..." The ending isn't the only part of that paragraph that got my attention. "But what about the other part? He's getting married?"

I can feel Tyler smile against my skin before he pulls away with a slightly pink tint to his cheeks. "Well, yeah. He's in love with Sean, and they're getting married. It seemed like the perfect way to end his story?"

"Oh yeah?" I turn sideways and pull Tyler up onto my bent leg. "Is that the perfect ending? A wedding?"

He shrugs but doesn't make eye contact. "Maybe not the ending forever...but that seems like a good start to a happy ending."

I can't keep away from him any longer. I capture his soft lip with my teeth and tug gently before diving in for a heated kiss. He's everything I could have hoped for, and knowing his happy ending is exactly what I want too just makes me love him even more. "I think so too."

"Really?" He slides off my lap, reaching for both of my hands. With his palms tightly grasping mine, he stares deeply into my eyes. "So you want that some day?"

I nod without breaking eye contact. "More than anything."

He pulls back with a slightly panicked look on his face. "Wait, we're not asking each other, right? This isn't a proposal or anything, is it?"

I laugh at his adorable panic. "No, when I propose, you'll know it."

His whole body relaxes, and he leans close to me again. "So you think might do that some day?"

"I think so." I know so. It's way too soon to do it now, but I've been thinking about it a lot lately.

"I love you, Joshua Douglas." Tyler lifts up on his knees and presses against my chest, pushing me flat on the couch. "And if you ever do, you'll make me the happiest man alive."

Unsure I can keep my emotions at bay, I don't say anything. I just kiss my man hard enough to assure him that he's already made me the happiest man alive. My fingertips are just sliding below the waistband of Tyler's sweatpants when my phone rings.

"Fuck." I quickly lift Tyler off my body and dig my phone out of my pocket. "Douglas here."

"Josh, get your ass back to the station." Chad sounds different than I've ever heard him. He's usually playful or calm. Occasionally, he's pissed off but he's never sounded like this. Afraid.

"What's going on?" I'm already walking to the door before he says the words that stop me in my tracks.

"Britney's dead. Dwight heard Harper crying by the back door and found her."

"I'll be there in ten." I turn to Tyler and reach out for him. "I'm bringing Ty."

Sorry for the cliffy. I don't usually do those, but I just didn't know how better to introduce _When The Bough Breaks_, Book Eight in the Mile High Romance Series.

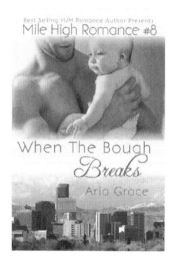

More M/M Romance books by Aria Grace:

Mile High Romance series

More Than Friends series

Promises Series
(M/M and M/F Contemporary)

Break Me Like a Promise (#1)

Trust Me Like a Promise (#2)

Keep Me Like a Promise (#3)

Real Answers Investigations series

Corner Office (#1)*

Soy Latte (#2)*

Cheers To That (#3)

Standalones

His Undoing (Gay For You)*

Winter Chill (First Time Gay)*

Escaping in Oz (College First Time)

*Also available as an audiobook

Learn more at www.AriaGraceBooks.com or become a kick ass fan and join my mailing list for updates and free book opportunities.

ariagracebooks@gmail.com

https://twitter.com/AriaGraceBooks

https://www.facebook.com/ariagracebooks

http://youtube.com/ariagracebooks

http://www.amazon.com/author/ariagrace

Made in the USA
Middletown, DE
18 November 2024

64901614R00146